ANDREW SCHRADER
BAD REALITIES

Bad People Publications

BAD REALITIES

For information, contact:
Andrew Schrader
HTTP://WWW.ANDREWJSCHRADER.COM

Bad People Publications
Editing by Karen S. Conlin
Cover photo and design by Jordan Harris
Cover title design by Hannah Nance
ISBN-13: 979-8-9874983-0-9

First Edition: 2023

Praise for *Bad Realities*

"While Schrader plays around with genres, it's all consistently disconcerting and scary stuff. Characters persistently wind up in harrowing circumstances or, as the title suggests, face some horrible, disturbing truth... the author casts a spell with sharp, concise prose and climaxes that will rattle most readers. Dark, indelible, and gleefully unsettling tales."

— Kirkus Reviews

Praise for *Escaping Midnight*

"★★★★★ Another weird and wonderful collection of compelling short stories. I would certainly suggest that if you have a vivid imagination, you definitely need to read this brilliant book with the lights on."

— Readers' Favorite

Praise for *What Goes On in the Walls at Night*

"★★★★★ Schrader's writing does much more than amuse. He urges us to acknowledge that while life is mind-boggling and frightening beyond belief, it's also fascinating as hell. Schrader has proven that even some of our nightmares are worth remembering."

— Red City Reviews

Also by Andrew Schrader

What Goes On in the Walls at Night

Vanish Into Midnight

Escaping Midnight

*Normalcy is an illusion: What is normal for the
spider is chaos for the fly.*

— CHARLES ADDAMS

***

*If, to Man, a cricket seems to hear with its legs, it
is possible that to the cricket, Man seems to walk
on his ears.*

— ANONYMOUS

Table of Contents

Preface 9

The Importance of Eating Ernest 17

Chop 25

Hondo Rane and the City of Illusion 28

Dogfight 63

I'm Ready to Affirm You Now, Gamma.....70

Seeds..79

Family 88

Man of Stone 95

Jack Nasty on the Wind 98

Lonely One...111

In The Trees (A Fairy Tale).......................124

The Floating Brain......................................134

Acknowledgements.....................................211

About the Author.......................................213

Preface

As we near the end of 2022, the country swerves headlong into mental illness. A dense fog of depression seems to be smothering my friends, my industry here in Los Angeles. Anxiety nips at all our heels like a foam-mouthed dog from hell.

Do you feel it, too?

Some blame the pandemic, a lingering collective grief from the previous two years. Or maybe it's the president's fault. The economy. Inflation. Our collective Pisces in the Sixth House.

They may play a part in all this. But I have another theory.

It has to do with machines.

MOST DAYS I WAKE UP AND (AFTER MEDITATING) immediately grab my phone. Sometimes I've committed the unforgivable sin of forgetting to charge it. It gasps on its last breath. I ask for its absolution.

I scroll for a while if I can, then sit down and turn on my TV. I usually watch YouTube, some combination of news and finance shows. I have a USB-powered reading light on the bookshelf to my right, and sometimes I forget to charge that as well. If so, I grab my little USB charger. Oh, I almost forgot my iPad. It tends to have very little battery left, because my lady and I like to lie in bed at night and watch some dumb show to help us stave off whatever internal demons we seem to be fighting at the time long enough to get a few hours of sleep. I usually have to plug it in several mornings a week if I want to browse Yahoo! Finance or check Zillow listings for homes I can't afford.

I go through much of my day like this: tending to my devices, charging my earbuds and computer. I love them. I can't live without them. I've conformed myself to their schedules, their nap times. And sometimes I find myself growing panicked when they run low on juice. Is there anything more pathetic?

My question is this: If I spend so much time caring for my machines, giving them life—then who's in charge, exactly? I like to tell myself that they serve me, that *I'm* using *them*. But is it true? Is a butler who tends to his master—drawing baths, preparing food, washing whites—really the boss?

SO, WHAT? YOU ASK. WHO CARES IF YOU USE YOUR DEVICES too much? Is there anything wrong with that? Isn't your life much better now that you're more connected, more informed, more prepared?

Good questions.

I just think they're the wrong ones to ask.

To be sold for mass production, machines must be reliable; they must run like clockwork, and each unit must work the same as any other. They are programmed to ignore the outside world, to focus on only the operations they're told to run. A smartphone doesn't remind you to feed your cat—unless you tell it to. It doesn't alert you to take your prostate medication—unless it is programmed to.

And most of us *do* program our machines, even when we aren't aware of it. We ask them to tell us when we've gotten enough steps, if we should try that new Thai restaurant, which hydro colon therapist in our area is the best.

We use machines to educate, to economize, to optimize. We tailor our podcasts, our videos, our algorithms for our every mood. Sometimes we even use them to screen out information, in order to stay "focused" or "productive."

Before we know it, we've developed a strange neurosis. Because we can't operate without our devices, and our devices can't operate without a charge, we become unconsciously anxious about their potential to die on us. How could we possibly live without them? Who will tell us what to do in case of an earthquake, a fire, a vote in Congress we don't agree with? Besides, disaster could strike at any time. We must be prepared. What to do if there's a shooting nearby? Should we hoard iodine pills in case of a nuclear fallout? Is our neighbor a closeted [Insert Political Party Here], and should we avoid her?

Fortunately, our trusty oracles have us covered. Google, for instance, has approximately 6,810,000 search results for "how to talk to your racist uncle." Apps tell us which foods came from dirty manufacturers, and which are secretly GMOs. We demand their advice, unaware that our reliance on them is creating more of the same anxiety that commands us to consult it for more advice! Try Googling "anxiety from devices"—I promise you'll find plenty of helpful information.

So we go along to get along and continue to scroll, perfecting our personal algorithms and deleting any potential unknowns from our lives as best we can.

But then something happens, something our devices didn't foresee, and we have no explanation, nothing to shield us from the void of a data-free world.

IN 2019, ON A SUNDAY MORNING, I WOKE UP FROM A nightmare. I don't remember the specifics, but I just *knew* my friend Marcus was in some kind of trouble. I was disturbed enough to tell my girlfriend about the dream. Eventually, I got up and went about my day.

Some days later, I logged into Facebook. Marcus's mother had posted that he was missing, and had been for a couple days.

The following week I learned that authorities had found his body. He'd apparently drowned himself. I didn't doubt the story, since he'd been struggling with schizophrenia for some time. Needless to say, I was upset and disturbed by the death of one of my oldest friends.

The unsettling part came next: He was pronounced to have died the morning I woke up from my dream that something horrible had happened to him.

NOW, ONE CAMP MIGHT SAY THAT IT WAS MARCUS LETTING me know he was leaving. Another will proclaim my dream was *completely* random. And yet another would say that although I wasn't conscious of it, I intuitively understood something was wrong with my friend, and my dream was simply good timing. Others may have their own theories.

I only know three things.

One, that my friend is gone, and I miss him.

Two, that no machine could have predicted or explained why I had that dream when I did.

Three, that my subconscious—that thing that lurks in the recesses of my mind—absolutely, positively, 100 percent wanted me to know.

I'M CONVINCED, TOO, OF SOMETHING ELSE: THAT THE subconscious in all of us is not happy with our fusing with the machine world.

In fact, it's very angry.

It's very angry with us for a very simple reason. We ignore it. We wave off its signals, its wisdom, its love of luck and randomness: those things that make little sense to the rational mind but which secretly direct our lives. The chance encounter on a plane to Phoenix resulting in a future marriage. The little voice in the back of your brain that illogically commands you to take one route to work over another. An inner feeling you can't explain, but which you just know is telling you that the old house you Airbnb'd in Fells Point in Baltimore is haunted. Why won't you listen?

We've used technology to optimize and control our lives so finely that we crowd out our subconscious. We supplant our inner wisdom with screens, pretending that if we cling hard enough we can control ourselves, our lives, the political process, our pesky neighbors with that tacky sign in their front yard.

One problem: Ignoring the subconscious doesn't work. First of all, there is no way to eliminate the unexplainable from our lives, no matter how much we make like ostriches and bury our heads in the dirt of Big Tech. Our subconscious isn't buying our line of bullshit that all we need is more data points to make informed and rational decisions. That is not the attitude of the human being; it is the worldview of a machine.

The subconscious, on the other hand, craves the unknown. It loves randomness. It is the enemy of the machine. And since we have fused with the machine, we have made enemies with our subconscious. So now it barks at us. It barks loudly. It causes anxiety. Yet, to calm our anxiety, we run back to our devices. What a pickle we're in!

Our "relationship" with the robots is more like Stockholm Syndrome. They are our captors, and we've fallen in love with them. We think like them. We believe that only new information is relevant; old information has already been ingested and digested and made *irrelevant*. That's the way of the machine, this insistence upon staying "up to date" and optimized. We remain on the lookout for some new Tik Tok video or Instagram Reel. *What do we think about the latest fad? What's your opinion on Problem X or Decision Y?* What is this mindless scrolling but an abortive attempt to snatch some kind of control back from the unknowns of life?

To say no to the machines is, to most people's thinking, to say no to progress. This is the way of the world now, they say. And we should always let go of the old and embrace the new. We should be optimizing, they say.

Maybe. But to optimize endlessly is to go insane. Sometimes to stay in place, or to meander, or even to go backward, is not actually to go backward. Sometimes backward, as Loren Eiseley wrote, is the only way to protect the human spirit.

The mechanical world of perpetual continuity is a vastly lonely and disquieting one. If everything can be "figured out" with more data, then our thoughts, feelings, imaginations, and even our lives do not matter much, do they? If so, then we are simply programmable automatons, not living, breathing gods who shit.

Can you think of anything more isolating and anxiety-provoking?

So what the hell does any of this have to do with what you're about to read? Have I really spent several pages outlining my latest Ted Talk?

I don't know what genres I write. I just ask the subconscious what it wants to say, and then I put it down on paper, by hand. I figure the rest will work itself out. My only request for the stories that follow is that you set aside your rational thinking, your analyzing and optimizing brain, and read them from your subconscious, where two people can actually meet. It's still a place where the machines can't reach, damn it, where novelty and chance are allowed to reign again from their proper thrones, barking orders at us from the backs of our skulls.

Besides, amid all this endlessly exhausting forward progress, someone has to stay behind and defend the subconscious. It deserves that much. So does Marcus.

Will you meet me there?

Can I count on you?

In constant terror,

Andrew Schrader

The Importance
of Eating Ernest

T HEY BRANG BODY IN AND GAVE TO ME.
"The flesh must be eaten to save the world,"
say Auntie. And the people brang another one.
And another. They give me, tell me to eat. Or else world
go boom-boom.

Billions go boom-boom.

I hungry. All the time. That is good. That is very
good. Else I could not eat it all. But I hungry. So I eat. I
eat it all.

"Tool! New tool!" I slap floor. "My cut-cut broken!"

Woman—Auntie—she say okay and go back to top
stairs. To kitchen. Light hurting my eyes. She take too

long. Door still open.

I hold hand over face. Block light because it hurts. My chains rattle. I hungry. Need my cut-cut to eat body.

So I wait.

Auntie waddle back and forth. I laugh. Hand me cut-cut. Look tired. Eyes darker than before last sleep. Not clean.

My heart go *thump-thump* for Auntie.

"They're all up there," say she. "Outside the house. All counting on you to keep eating."

"Only one of me!" say I. "No need to count." I throw hands up; she make no sense.

She smile and sit down. Groan. Carry bodies downstairs hard work. Carry them all the time. Many, many bodies. For many, many sleeps she bring bodies.

I play with cut-cut. It sharp. Good for cutting body down here.

I get start cut while Auntie rest.

Her job hard.

Mine easy.

I just eat.

But then—

Knock, knock. On door.

Auntie look scared. Her heart go *bang-bang*. Eyes tell me afraid.

"Never mind," say she. "I always tell you too much. I'll get in trouble. I'll be back again later. Just know that I love you. Now be a good boy and keep eating."

"Okay," say I.

She waddle away. Answer door up top and go out.

No more knockie.

I EAT MAN. MEAT BETWEEN KNEE AND BUTTOCKS TASTE

best. My favorite part. Juicy. So much juicy.

Eat man take a while. Some sleeps needed. Five fingers worth. To eat him all.

Auntie get nervous when take five fingers worth. Say people upstairs "restless" and be angry with her when take so long. She ask me go faster.

"I go fast as I can," say I. Feel hurt by words. Nobody of them eat so much human! Like to see them eat so much human!

She say it okay and pat my head. Make heart *thump-thump*.

She take box of bones I give her and go back upstairs.

I hear noises when she go up. People happy. Yell like "Yay!"

I make some sound like "Yay!"

But it not sound like them.

Two sleeps later. Auntie come down. Drag new body down stairs. Man body.

He look same old as me. I ask if he same old as me.

"No," say she. "And you shouldn't ask those things."

I want know. I cross arms. Hurt my heart, did she.

Auntie smile at me. "Okay," say she, "He was thirty-one years old."

I excite. "He same old as me?"

"No, Ernest," say she. "You're thirty-three."

She tell me, thirty-three. Each year many, many sleeps. Thousands of sleeps in thirty-three years.

I whistle at that. So many sleeps!

"How many people do sleeps?" ask I.

"Every one of them," say she. "Everyone around the world. Many people. Billions. All kept alive because of you. Because you eat the flesh, they live on."

She pat my head and go.

My heart feel good again.

I eat man of almost-same-old-as-me faster than the last one.

For her. For Auntie.

I BE IN MY SLEEPS AND EYES CLOSED. I LOOK AT CAGE. I always look at cage in sleeps time. Animals that move in big thumps. Other animals swim in big drink-drink cups.

But then, no more cage. No more animals.

I open eyes. Auntie in my face. Wake me from sleeps.

"Ssh," say she. "Don't make a sound."

She unhook my chains. Arms feel free. Legs are loose.

"I'm taking you out of here," say she. "They can't keep you locked up forever—the world be damned."

She put arm around me, help me to walk.

"They've all gone away for a few hours," say she. "And I'm taking you where they can't find you."

My heart big for Auntie. I follow her anywhere she want. But it beat fast when I think she leave me.

"Don't be scared," say she. "I'll protect you as best I can. Even if the world does end when you stop eating, it's not right. It's not right at all. You're still a human being, goddamnit."

We go up stairs. One at a time. Heart full and good for Auntie.

At door top and—

We push open.

Many hands and much noise. People came back early —too much before time good.

Auntie yell at them!

She hang onto me! I hang onto her and make mean

face at others!

"Traitor!" yell they. "You want us all to die?"

I yell for Auntie. She yell for me.

But her hand leave mine. They take her hand from mine. They hands swallow her up, and she disappear. *Where Auntie?!*

I want them dead! I want Auntie back! I fight them. I bite and kick and scratch at them. They take Auntie. I want Auntie. I give them all I got in fight!

But it no good! They take me, take me down to chains.

Many hands put chains back on wrists, on legs. I can't see their faces. They stupids. I want them dead. I want—

But someone hit me on head . . . and sleeps come. . . .

A new someone bring bodies now. Not Auntie. Ugly man. Hurts eyes. I yell for him to bring Auntie back. He make face-grin.

I hungry though. I very hungry.

First body brings is small boy. I eat fast. I so hungry.

I hear yells of "Yay!" from upstairs. They like I eat. Eat save them, save peoples. All the peoples. Billions of them.

I still hungry. Man bring baby to eat.

I eat.

They yell "Yay!"

I miss Auntie. Water eyes for Auntie.

After I no sleeps, big ugly man bring new body.

I crawl to body.

I look at body.

I no believe it.

The water eyes are back for me.
Auntie look up at me.
She!
I hug Auntie. I yell "Yay!" like the people upstairs. Auntie get many smooches. Many hugs.
But—
Auntie not move.
She stiff, not blink her eyes.
I sit back. I watch.
Auntie, she . . .
They bring me Auntie, *like this?*
She . . . dead?
They bring me dead Auntie like other bodies they want me to—
Eat?
I look down.
They want me eat Auntie?
To save world?

I sit through one sleeps. I cannot sleeps.
I no want to.
I will not eat her. I no eat her. I refuse.
Now I hear not yells of "Yay!"
I hear yells of mean-face.
But I do not care.
I no eat Auntie.

Two sleeps pass.
I still no eat.
I WILL NOT.
They bring down other bodies. Try other bodies.
No!
They yell at me. To eat Auntie. To eat something.

But no!

I WILL NOT.

With no Auntie, I no live. No want to live.

I tell them so!

Sleeps later, a few sleeps. I think the thought.

The changing thought.

Make decision.

To eat again.

Yes. That is the idea.

Eat again.

I have it. I have best idea.

So I begin to eat.

They yell of "Yay!"

I hear them yell of "Yay!"

Little do they know—

I near finish second leg.

Second leg already.

My leg.

I eat me.

To teach them. Teach them lesson. Lesson of no more eats. No more eats of anyone.

When I gone, they go gone. *Boom-boom.*

I hate them.

I hurt. Hurt turns to sleeps. I feel sleeps coming. I go sleeps very soon.

Forever sleeps. Join Auntie in forever sleeps.

Heart go *thump-thump* for Auntie.

I miss Auntie.

Water eyes for Auntie.

As I go sleeps . . .

I hear them . . .

The screams . . .

Up there . . .
All them . . .
They gave me, tell me to eat. Or else world go *boom-boom*.
So I eat for them.
I show them, alright.
They go *boom-boom*.
Billions of them.
Goodbye.

Chop

THE COUPLE WATCHED FROM THE RESTAURANT across the street. The line was three blocks long and growing longer by the minute.

Angie craned her neck. "I can't see the end of it anymore." She turned back to her husband. "The news said over a million people have already gotten it done. You know Lee from work? She did it at home."

Edgar let his coffee cup clatter on the table. "*At home?*"

His wife nodded, eyebrows raised. "People don't want to wait in clinic lines. I mean, look how long this one is."

"Crazy."

"It certainly is." She sipped her tea, glancing around the cafe. Only a few tables were full this Sunday, much emptier than normal. Everyone was getting the procedure done.

"No one can explain it," she said. "Why it's

happening, I mean. Why do you think it's happening?"

Edgar shrugged. "Who knows why anyone does anything these days."

"Fads catch on for all kinds of reasons, I guess?"

"I guess."

They drank and browsed their phones. They tried not to watch the line across the street and the people who disappeared beyond the heavy metal doors.

"Here." Angie handed him her phone with the article on it. "What do you think of this?"

Edgar read. It seemed to make sense to him. He told Angie so. Then he read another piece, a different explanation. That seemed to make sense, too. He told Angie so.

Across the room, a woman stood. She appeared to be in her mid-thirties, wearing a sweatshirt off one shoulder, with a picture of a teddy bear on the front.

"You're so brave!" She clapped for the man who sat across the booth from her.

The man turned to the waiter and asked for something in hushed tones.

The waiter returned a moment later with a large knife.

The woman was already crying tears of joy. "I'm so happy for you," she exclaimed, clasping her hands together in front of her chest.

Edgar rolled his eyes and sipped his coffee.

"Are they really going to do it *here?*" Angie asked.

The man across the restaurant handed his girlfriend the knife. He set his hand flat on the table. The waiter stood back and watched.

The girl swung the knife down, chopping off the last three fingers in one swipe. The force sent them skittering across the floor. One of them came to rest a few inches from Edgar's shoe. Frowning, he turned back to the window and kept drinking.

When the chopping had finished, the girlfriend paid the waiter and left. Her boyfriend's arms and legs lay on the floor. You could swim in the blood. The man had long since passed out. If he wasn't dead yet, he would be soon.

Angie turned to Edgar. "I read that the paramedics have been disbanded. No one is asking for them anymore."

"Sounds about right," he said.

The waiter cleaned up the body parts and the blood, and pretty soon the booth was good as new.

When they had finished, Edgar left some cash on the table, including a generous tip.

Stepping onto the sidewalk, they gazed at the line to get chopped, which was even longer now. It seemed like a million people were out today.

Angie squinted in the sun. "It's strange, isn't it?"

"It certainly is."

"And why do you think it's happening?"

"Beats me," he said. "Fads catch on for all kinds of reasons."

"I suppose you're right." She sighed. "Okay, then. Should we get to it?"

"Absolutely."

Joining hands, they walked to the back of the line.

Hondo Rane and the City of Illusion

Chapter I

O F THE TWO ROADS INTO TARKAGEN, HE CHOSE THE one with more hills and valleys, the one he had preferred as a boy. He remembered every rise and fall of the many knolls, every turn of the way; surprisingly, little had changed in the twenty-five years he'd been gone. From the swamps still drifted the croaks of throaty frogs the size of a man's head, the ones he used to catch long ago with his brother.

His sandals slapped the packed dirt, the road worn over many thousands of years of Bonaryus rule. He carried his sword, his pack, his ax, and basic supplies. The raven that Vail had sent flew behind him, lazily scanning its surroundings as they moved deeper into the woods.

Cresting over the final hill, he glimpsed the majestic city. Something felt oddly vacant about it all, even from a distance. He'd traveled far in his journeys, but never back here, where he'd once called home.

On his way down the hill, he caught the scent of honeysuckle drifting across the land. He had only encountered it twice since leaving Tarkagen: once, on the high seas while scouting off Atlantis for the emperor of Sowell, and the other, strangely enough, upon learning of the death of his brother, Garson.

This second occurrence was the reason for his return.

As the city came into fuller view, the raven squawked twice and flew ahead. They'd meet again at home, later. Hondo would easily find his way back from here.

Although he was a barbarian, and battle gave him no pause, his palms sweated at the thought of entering his childhood home. It wasn't the mission at hand that frightened him; the incursion and stealthy escape to come troubled him little. Instead, it was the dim and unsettling sense—gnawing at him just below the level of consciousness—that soon he would have to face himself, finally, for the first time.

Chapter 2

Indeed, Tarkagen had changed. The fishmongers who once lined the street had been replaced by jugglers and musicians begging for change. The opulent towers housing the citizens and overlooking the town square had fallen into ill repair; hunks of mortar around the window frames had disintegrated, leaving gaping holes where the immaculate stained glass had once been.

Hondo pulled his cloak tighter, protecting his sword and ax from any wandering eyes as he crossed the busy street. Best to keep things hidden wherever possible. Keep the enemy on their toes; give nothing away. That's what Hondo had learned the hard way some ten or twelve years prior in the war for the Majeelan Peninsula, when he'd gotten the scar that ran from his right eye down past his jaw like an elongated tear. It was there, in those battles, that he'd learned how to fight, how to kill. And, if need be, how to die admirably.

"The lost Elixir of Youth!" A young woman of fourteen yelled into a large cone made of pig leather. Her voice rang out over the square. "It's here, somewhere in the city! The emperor has offered a thousand sconce for its return!"

Hondo read the sign next to the girl. Bearing the emperor's signature at the bottom, it indeed advertised a tidy reward for the retrieval of the vial of the Elixir of Youth, an image of which was hand-drawn on the board. A thousand sconce, he thought. A tidy sum. Little doubt why the emperor, over eighty winters now, would do everything in his power to retrieve it. Hondo let himself ponder the implications. In the emperor's hands, with the extra time the elixir would afford him, who knew what untold damage could be done. The emperor had already tried expanding his reach well past the negotiated territory to the east. His military was spread thin, but the soldiers were well trained and in control of key ports.

Uneasy, Hondo moved on. For a quarter league he saw mostly magicians and, sparingly, sellers of fruit and meat. Most of the fruit was already rotting; the meat, turning rancid. Strangely, nobody seemed to mind. Most people were focused on having fun, enjoying performances from the illusionists, or playing novoo, a popular card game. They bet pence or tobacco; he could tell by the smell of the latter it was of bad quality. This was good for him; he could trade his fine Atlantean tobacco if he needed to.

A few blocks farther, he came upon an illusionist with several small, round mirrors nestled between his splayed fingers. The hunched man sprinted up to Hondo. Holding the mirrors up to his face, the illusionist reflected six tiny images of the barbarian.

"Stay here, my big friend!" he cried out. "And watch!"

Light from an upstairs window found the rightmost mirror in his hand. Catching the reflected light with his left hand, and reflecting it back yet again, and again, the illusionist created a prism.

The prism expanded. To Hondo it seemed as though the outside world was receding beyond the mirrors and the images within. Whether it was the refraction of light that produced the magic trick, Hondo couldn't say, but after a few seconds his image transcended the mirrors— or, rather, he went *inside* them.

"An optical illusion, sir!" the trickster said. "Look at yourself. What do you see?"

At first, he saw what anyone else would see of him: a broad-shouldered, lantern-jawed giant with a week's stubble and bright blue eyes. But the longer he looked, the more mesmerized he became. His face began to change; his scar receded into the skin. His hair, tangled and filthy, straightened and fell across his face like that of a young man. The longer he looked, the more civilized his appearance turned. In fact, he realized, he was going back in time. He grew younger in the image, his body shrinking by the second. Then, an older man began to materialize beside him. He rested a hand on young Hondo's shoulder. A shudder went through the giant, an icy chill running up his back, as the man tightened his grip.

No, it couldn't be *him*.

The illusionist yanked the mirrors away. "Just a taste, sir. You'll need five pence to keep the illusion going."

Hondo blinked, snapping himself out of the vision. He felt dizzy. His heart raced. It took a few breaths to shake seeing his father like that.

"What is that?" he asked. "How does it work?"

"A magician never reveals his secrets," the man said. "But I can tell you the effect. It takes the viewer back into his deepest memories, good and bad. To those times in one's youth that are forever embedded in his shadow self. To relive, over and over again."

"An artificial elixir of youth," the barbarian said, more to himself than the magician.

"Yes." The man's chest puffed up proudly. "In fact, while the emperor awaits the retrieval of the elixir, he lives his days in the mirrors. As does most of the city. These mirrors. *My* mirrors."

Hondo nodded, not yet recovered. It was a miraculous illusion. When the trickster again offered him the mirrors for five pence, Hondo waved him away and moved on.

Some memories were best left untouched.

Chapter 3

The stairs up to his childhood home were steeper than he remembered. The home's exterior was carved into rock. You'd never know that behind the heavy oak door lodged in sandstone lay so many memories, so much pain, and so much hidden treasure.

He pushed the door open. The place had retained the same musty smell he remembered from boyhood. He went in and entered a narrow hallway that sloped down. Stone floors led into the main antechamber. There were no decorations, only austere rock, save the chandelier hanging from the fifteen-foot ceiling. It had been crafted by his third-last grandfather, Tomtoro of Arkadin. It was priceless. Too bad they'd soon have to leave it behind.

In the main living area, a fire crackled in the hearth. Set for him, he presumed.

He stepped through the hallway in back and into the room where he slept as a boy. He gazed upon the bed, the rocking chair in the corner, the small bookshelf to its right. It still held such titles as *Fairy Tales of Rockhound* and *Evander the Great,* fantasy and adventure books he'd read many, many times huddled away here, hiding from the others, finding respite in stories rather than people.

"The estranged one returns," came a raspy voice. Gripping his crutch, the old man stepped into the room. Light from the lone window wrapped him gently. One eye protruded from his head like a stubborn nail in a piece of wood. The other was tightly bandaged over.

"Vail," Hondo said. "Many moons it's been."

The two men smiled softly, and each gazed upon how the other had changed.

"You got my message." Vail nodded toward the raven, who appeared to be sleeping on the wooden perch in the wall. "His name is Madness. A constant companion in a place like this, with few windows and little light. A man needs someone to converse with. Either his own madness or a bird. Might as well be a bird. Anyway, take off your cloak. Let's eat."

They dined in the heart of the house, in the room to the east of the big antechamber. Vail had procured a dinner of pork and pickled eggs, though the grade of meat was well below the quality of what Hondo ate on the road.

Hondo looked up at the charcoal portrait of his brother, Garson, that hung over the fireplace. To its left was the sketch of his father's face; to the right, Hondo's. Garson and his father looked very much alike: same high cheekbones and slender face. Hondo's long, sloping forehead contrasted greatly. They seemed hardly related. Hondo looked away and tore into his pork.

"I'm sorry to bring you back for this," Vail said. "I know you and Garson hadn't spoken in some time."

"If not for you, I would not have come at all."

"And I thank you."

Hondo chewed thoughtfully, taking several moments to bring himself to ask the question.

"How did my brother die?"

Vail cleared his throat. "I believe his problems with money started it. Running up various debts over time. The past ten years or so have seen many schemes in the city. People are growing more and more desperate to turn a profit. Your brother bought into bad partnerships. He was unable to cope."

"Unable to cope. How?"

"Garson took to the drink more and more. The worse the news he received, the more he drank. Eventually . . ."

"It killed him."

"You could say that." Vail set his fork down and looked Hondo in the eye. "He threw himself out the window. By the time I found him, it was too late. There was nothing I could do. No spell to consider."

Hondo took this in. He supposed he should feel sadness or regret. But he felt nothing at all.

"It's not your fault," he said. "Every man chooses his own path." There was a pop from the fire. Hondo peered into it, deep in thought, his mind retracing vague memories. Another pop brought him out. "Who would have thought it would be me still alive, of us three Rane men? Certainly not Father."

Vail sighed. "Hondo. Enough with your misery and martyrdom." When he had commanded the giant's attention, he said, softer now, "Do you remember what I told you the day you left home?"

Hondo shook his head.

"I told you that you were born a warrior. I told you that you cannot fight what you are. I told you how your father tried, how he fought what you were. He couldn't bring himself to live with a barbarian in his bloodline. In the end, he fought himself." He leaned in across the table, the firelight glinting in his good, uncloudy eye. "He and your brother are dead because they lived in illusions of their own. Just like the rest of the city. They were not immune to its charms."

Vail waved his hand. "Even now I can see it in your eyes. The fear you carry. Like them, you live in a delusion."

"What delusion?"

"That you can be something other than yourself. You are a barbarian. And there is no shame in it." Vail pointed a gnarled finger. "Remember this, Hondo Rane: You will never win the battle of life, not until you let go of such falsehoods."

CHAPTER 4

AFTER DINNER, THEY WENT BACK TO HONDO'S ROOM. VAIL walked to the far wall, inserted his fingers in the gap between two chest-high stones, and turned them. Hondo heard something inside the wall go *clunk*—and then a small door opened in the stone facade.

Vail reached into the hole and raised the lid on a chest that sat inside. He removed the vial and handed it to Hondo. It was heavier than the barbarian had expected.

"This is it, then," Hondo said. "The Elixir of Youth."

"Three hundred years it's been handed down," Vail said. "Now yours to safeguard."

Hondo examined the vial. It was a small but heavy thing; in fact, the liquid inside was not the weight of water, but the weight of gold. "There are announcements across the city," he told Vail. "The emperor offers a large reward for its retrieval."

"Yes. The man's gone batty with age. For years he's been convinced that the elixir is hiding somewhere within the city walls. Obsessed, now. Just last moon he ransacked five homes."

Hondo raised an eyebrow. "Have his soldiers come here?"

"Many times." Vail leaked a smile. "But they've never entered."

"Why not? What secret do you possess?"

"Oh, a simple potion poured at the base of the door. As the soldiers pass by, they are filled with feelings of homesickness. They equate this place with their childhood homes. Since they can't possibly imagine anything so sinister in the places of their youth, they find it impossible to believe anyone would hide an illegal potion here!"

"You make them one with their emotions." Hondo grinned. "That is the way of the beasts."

"They *are* beasts, my friend."

Hondo turned back to admire the false wall. But it was then he caught a glimpse of the pockmarks in the wall where the chains had once been latched. His heart thumped; he reflexively massaged his wrists where the scars still bore his secrets. In his mind's eye he saw his father, ratcheting the chains tighter and tighter, preparing the whip.

"The restraints were removed many moons ago." Vail set a gentle hand on his shoulder, snapping him out of the past. "Nothing to fear now."

Hondo nodded and waited for his nerves to calm. Those memories hadn't surfaced in decades; he found it extraordinary that they could have such an impact on him. It was he, he reminded himself, the barbarian who had defeated the wizards of Krishnapur, who had stormed the towers of the Clamath Deserts. Surely these memories could not affect him so much.

And yet, there was nothing he could do but leave the room and let Vail prepare him some calming tea. Not even a barbarian can always forge a clean road through the terrors of his mind alone.

"WITH GARSON GONE, WE CANNOT KEEP THE VIAL HERE." Vail handed Hondo his tea. "I cannot stay alone anymore, in this stone castle. It's time I left the city. And if I leave, the vial must come with me."

"Why didn't Garson sell the elixir to the emperor?" Hondo asked. "No doubt it would have ended his money troubles."

"It's quite simple, really. He didn't know about it."

"You never told him?" Hondo's voice rose.

"I have served the Ranes for forty years, Hondo. Your father gave me the elixir to protect, not to sell. Had I told Garson, he would have sold it. Therefore, I did not tell him."

"You're right. Forgive me."

Vail softened. "Think nothing of it." He thought for a moment. "You must understand: The emperor can never be allowed to possess the vial. Though he is weak, and has already run the city into the ground, he still controls vast resources. He has yet to tap the help of some of his partner cities. His soldiers are scattered, yes, but they are powerful. With the elixir, he would not only revive himself, but the other aging emperors as well. He would take all they would give for just a few drops. And they would give everything.

"You must remember that his ambitions know no bounds. His wrath is measureless. Time is the only thing scarcer than gold—and to gain more of it he would trade every soldier and ounce of the yellow metal he can. Once he consolidates his power, he will control, by force, every resource in the region.

"No, *nobody* can take control of the elixir. And yet . . .

the elixir cannot be destroyed. For thousands of years it has been shielded from man, and it must continue to be protected for the next many thousands. We have no choice but to carry this burden now, you and I, until we reach our destination, where it can be stored safely.

"I could never trust your father or brother with this task. I believe they were fated to die first. The gods wanted it. It's how it was supposed to be. For you are pure of heart, Hondo, and impervious to the schemes and machinations of the civilized mind. Fate has chosen you, so it is you who must lead us out."

Vail's one good eye bored into the barbarian. "And be warned. The elixir's powers are great. It draws men to it. It whispers to them. Once we set foot outside this house, the emperor will come for it. His foot soldiers will be like men possessed. As you said; like beasts, they will become one with their emotions."

Hondo's eyes narrowed. "Then I will crush them in the ring of combat."

"I'm sure you will. Now, get some rest. In the morning, you'll get supplies. And tomorrow night, we ride."

Vail blew out the candle, casting them into darkness.

Chapter 5

the wheezing of the flame
a crack of the whip
the young boy flinches
skinny and scarred, he hides in the shadows
from the figure, hulking, cruel, lording,

waiting. . . .
    pinning the child's arms above his head
            fingers grasping chains
      clinking, clanking
        locking his wrists
           and the whip strikes again—

Chapter 6

Hondo woke mid-run across the room, his hand behind his back but finding no sword there. The hiss of the fire and the roar of his child self from the dream echoed between his ears—but he was awake.

Crouching in the corner, the hulking barbarian panted for breath, his skin sticky and glistening. The latticework of ancient scars decorating his back flared, red-hot, like molten steel.

He had thought the dreams had left him for good. Now that he'd returned to Tarkagen, they'd returned as well.

It was still hours before morning. He tried to sleep. It proved fruitless. He lay in bed and gazed out the window, knowing not what to feel or think.

At dawn, he got dressed and breakfasted on a bowl of steaming barley mash that Vail had left for him by the hearth, then went to the stone balcony that overlooked the eastern portion of the city and beyond to the ocean. The early sun made the place pleasant and warm, heating the stones and creating a bath of light. He removed his pants and lay on his back, rolling up on his spine, legs curling over his torso, so the sun shone on his manhood and arse. "Sunning the beast," his fellow soldiers called it. It provided energy and warmth to those parts most men hide. Hondo was a warrior, a barbarian, and as he lived unlike town folk in other ways, he was novel in matters of health and sustenance, too.

Afterward, he trekked into town for food and supplies. Many years he'd spent roaming in the dark wood, absent from the affairs of townsfolk, searching for virtuous battles and jobbing for gold coins. He found the exposure of walking through town irritating at best. There was a gnawing sense of being watched, of nakedness. The emperor was still on the hunt for the elixir, and Hondo could not afford attracting attention.

He went dressed in an old cloak, like a poor man. His height and weight he could not hide, but perhaps he could play off as a grotesque, one of those freaks he once saw at a carnival as a young boy. He used a walking stick. Hunching over would support his ruse. For good measure, he slipped on an eyepatch, which would help him play the part of a large but doddering fool.

The quality of goods in town was abysmal. Sneering men in capes hawked rotten food, pork and beef drained of all color. He managed to find some decent gray polyroot, though an examination of the coins he received as change confirmed some of his suspicions about the state of his childhood home.

Tarkagen, a mighty hub of the Northland, had once contained vast deposits of iron, steel, and rare metals, which the emperor had sold to other cities to fund his own. Over time, two classes of citizens emerged. The first was the mining class; the other, the ruling class. One became very rich, the other stayed very poor. However, both began to consume trinkets and illusions they imported from conquered kingdoms. Entertainment became the main engine of commerce.

Over twenty winters, the population demanded more and more novelties. By then, the emperor had run the city into exorbitant debts that could not be repaid. The solution to their money problems had been to slowly replace the gold in the dinars with other, less expensive metals that were more readily available in the outer colonies.

Indeed, when Hondo bit one of the dinars, he guessed it comprised no more than 5 percent gold, the rest likely being a mixture of lead and copper.

Paying back old debts with degraded money seemed to have worked for Tarkagen . . . for a while. But then the prices of fresh fruit, pork, and lamp oil went so high that only the richest could afford them. In turn, the farmers and producers, aided by the alchemists in the Tarkagen Temple, devised new ways to cut corners. Sugar was replaced with the sweet but semi-toxic oils of the honey bush. The thick, black coffee the city was famous for became suffused with synthetic bitters. The sandstone that had supported many of Tarkagen's original structures was mixed with round stone, a plentiful substance that brittled quickly. It was that combination which produced the half-eaten citadels Hondo had spied upon entering the city.

In these ways, Tarkagen was able to maintain the semblance of normalcy, even as its foundation was slowly being chipped away.

"Hondo?" A voice called out.

The giant turned. A bow-legged man with a leathery complexion stood there.

Recognizing him quickly, Hondo looked away.

"Hondo Rane," the man said. "I thought that was you. The prodigal son returns, eh?"

The barbarian made a quick calculation. He could either continue ignoring him and risk drawing suspicion, or—

"Morlon Banchek." Hondo, milking a limp, hobbled over to him and shook his hand. "Greetings. Long time."

"Imagine my surprise when out on my morning walk, I spy an old friend back from battle. You aren't in a hurry, I hope? Time for a drink with your childhood friend?"

Hondo protested. "Apologies, but I must get back home—"

"Nonsense." Flashing a toothy grin, Morlon clapped a hand on Hondo's back and began leading him away. "I insist."

The tavern was dark and small. Men, hunching over their spirits, mumbled to themselves in dazed apathy. Some played card games like twistle or bashett. Many illegal deals were made in places like this.

They ordered grog and remembered old times. Hondo had already decided to leave after one drink; to go any sooner would only arouse suspicion. He and Morlon had trained together in the Emperor's Academy until they were sixteen, and those childhood bonds are hard to break. In spite of his anxiety, Hondo found he was mildly enjoying the conversation. In a place of so many poor memories, there were some good ones, too.

As Hondo finished his first mug, a melee broke out across the tavern involving a young woman and her husband. Casting his hand off her shoulder, she leapt from her chair and stormed out. The man stayed seated for a moment, no doubt embarrassed. Saving face, he sighed and picked up her chair, and as he turned to go, he caught Morlon's three-fingered wave.

He stopped short, his face dropping. Then he nodded to Morlon and returned the city salute, which was holding a hand with its fingers straight as a board, vertically between the eyes, so the palm split one's vision. He quickly left. Morlon turned back to Hondo.

He had given the salute of the emperor's Command.

Hondo sipped his drink and made no expression, though his heart began to thump a bit louder than he would have liked.

"That's Ravi," Morlon said. "And his wife, Eudora." He leaned in close to Hondo, his eyebrows raised, as if to impart some secret. His breath smelled like lamb that had been stripped off the bone a month prior. "By the emperor's decree, they are to surrender half their crops. Ravi will not refuse, but Eudora wants him to stand up to the emperor, to be a warrior, to fight back, *to be a man.*"

He leaned back and sipped his drink. "The woman will not win out."

"You work for the emperor, then? That's how you know such intimate details?"

Morlon grinned. "As the Emperor's Hand, I deal with all such intimate details."

They met gazes then, and Hondo did not look away. He knew he could display no fear or trepidation.

The Emperor's Hand, then. The confidant. The one who handled all matters of internal and external security. Who knew all the secrets. Who, no doubt, had been leading the hunt for the elixir all this time.

Hondo Rane was sitting with the one man he must

avoid.

"You've done well for yourself," the barbarian said, raising his refreshed mug of grog. "To your success."

"And to yours," Morlon said. They clinked cups. "Tell me, old friend, why have you graced Tarkagen with your return?"

"As the Hand, you must have known my brother, Garson."

"Of course. I heard of his passing. That's why you're here?"

"'Tis."

"Picking something up, I presume." Morlon looked away, as if to disarm him. He casually stirred his drink. "Something of importance?"

"Our servant, Vail. He's old and becoming infirm. Soon he'll be incapable of caring for himself. He wishes to move elsewhere, off the stone mountain."

"So he'll stay with you, eh? On the road, half-blind and horsed?"

"There's a home some fifty leagues from here. He will be comfortable there."

Morlon's eyes stabbed the giant. He was half Hondo's size and half as strong, yet twice as nasty. Hondo cleared his throat and sipped his grog, hoping to appear disinterested in his companion's reaction.

Morlon sat back and pulled a lemon from his pocket. He quickly stripped the skin and sliced a bit off. He appeared to be thinking.

"Sorry to see your eye a-missing," he said. "What's the story of that?"

"Oh." Hondo's hand went instinctively to his eyepatch. "A knife fight in South Bellington. Nasty scrabble."

"Of the many wounds I've seen," Morlon said, "those to the eye are the most horrible." He took a long pull from his cup and burped. "May I have a look?"

"At my eye?"

"Occipital damage can be severe, though I know of a doctor in town, the finest, who is only too happy to help treat it and provide a false eye."

"I'm afraid not. I do not like showing my wound."

"Come now, don't be bashful. I've seen it all." He reached across the table. "Was it a gouge or a swipe—"

In reflex, Hondo's hand lashed out. Quick to anger, primed by years of combat, he reacted. His fingers wrapped around the man's arm, wrenching him out of his chair and sending him sprawling across the floor.

In a flash, he realized his mistake. He hooked a hand around Morlon's shoulder and helped him to his feet, apologizing in haste.

"You dare strike the Emperor's Hand?" Morlon staggered back a few steps, dazed.

Hondo kneeled. "My humblest apologies," he said, eyes to the floor. The tavern guests gawked. They'd all seen a big one-eyed lunk strike the Hand, and would swear to it if necessary. "I reacted. I did not think. I am simply ashamed of my deformity. Of course, if you'd like to see this hole in my head, I am happy to show it to you. I do not deserve your sympathy, my Hand."

He waited, head bowed, for a response, deliberately exposing the back of his neck, offering his head, should the Hand request to lop it off.

Hondo cursed himself. The eyepatch. It was too clean, too neat. His story would never hold up to scrutiny, certainly not that of the Emperor's Hand. He should have dirtied it somewhat, put some wear around its edges, to better suit his tale about South Bellington.

Morlon stood silent. No doubt he was turning facts over in his beast-trap of a mind. The huge man stayed where he was, head bowed, staring at his old friend's feet.

A hand came to rest almost gently on the back of Hondo's head. "It's all right. Have no fear. I know you meant nothing by it. You were merely acting out of fear that I would react harshly to your eye—or lack thereof. In the future, however, your pre-judgment of my reaction is your own problem, is that understood?"

"Yes, my Hand."

"Rise."

Hondo did. Morlon had the look of a contented cat.

"I am still buying your drinks," the captain said. "Go on, go home. Perhaps we shall meet again soon."

Hondo nodded and hurried out. He glanced back only once, as he passed the window that peered into the tavern. Morlon was standing there, eating his lemon, still watching the barbarian, only now he was no longer smiling.

Chapter 7

In town, Hondo quickly finished gathering the rest of their supplies. He felt eyes on him; as an expert tracker, he knew when things were not all what they seemed to be. Still, it was important to appear at ease. If anyone was watching, it was best they thought him unaware. So he made a few more stops than usual, hoping to catch a spy in the act while taking in more of the sights.

Tricks. Mirages. Spectacles. Tarkagen had not been nicknamed the City of Illusion for nothing. He marveled at the amount of phantasm, the intricacies of the sideshows. There was Miraculous Mary, a wafer-thin lady with bulging eyes and stringy brown hair, who levitated off a stone mantel, after sweeping the ground in a circle to demonstrate that there was no hidden rope with which to raise her.

Then there was the swarthy man with four goats, who made each disappear and reappear in turn with the *woosh* of his wool blanket to the *oohs* and *aahs* of the audience.

The delight he took in the sights and sounds turned swiftly to shame. He felt like a child again, and in thinking about his childhood, he invariably recalled the insults hurled at him for his failure to understand the subjects that came easy to the other children.

He kicked a heavy stone. It skittered down an empty alley. He did not like brooding on the past, which led to ruminating about his father. His father, who had shamed him for his stature, who wished to erase the barbarian line in his blood. Garson had been born good; Hondo, a disgrace. He never did have the right mind, not for numbers or politics or money.

In those days, Hondo hid from family and friends, ensconcing himself in blankets at home and in large, bulky clothing at school. It wasn't until he left Tarkagen, after that final fight with his father, that he found some advantage in his physique. Barbarian work, like running rescue missions or protecting the Kthalekian princess during her escape from the Castle of the Ruinous Scar, had made him a thing of legends . . . just not at home. To these civilized men, he was a brute with no class. But out there, in the world of witchcraft and wizardry and ugly things that scurry at night, he was a champion.

If only he felt that way now.

It seemed impossible in this city, this miserable place of illusion.

Lost in himself, he ascended the staircase home. Had he kept his presence of mind, he might have noticed the three men in cloaks drenched in shadow standing off the stone road watching him.

Thankfully, he had Vail who, having the sorcerer's sense for malfeasance, was already preparing for the worst.

Chapter 8

Vail sat in stony silence until Hondo had finished his story.

"They'll be watching the front of the house," Vail said. "So tonight we shall leave out the back."

"You're sure they suspect us?" Hondo asked.

"Of a more murderous villain than Morlon Banchek, I know none. Childhood friend or not, he would have had troops here by now, you striking him like that. No, you cannot underestimate men like him. The only reason to let you live is to ensnare you later. Given that he's been tasked with finding the elixir and stopping its leaving the city by some entrusted hand, we must assume that he's fixed on us now. No, we leave tonight, and out the back." His cloak brushed the halls as he rushed to finish gathering his things.

Hondo gritted his teeth, his face growing crimson.

But there was no time to waste feeling sorry for himself or beating himself up for his mistake. He filled his pack with food, poultices, and gold dinars. The elixir he kept in a pouch secured tightly to his belt.

As for the potions, Vail had already crafted a pack made of sheepskin. When unrolled, it displayed various powders, tinctures, a small mortar and pestle, and a vial of sainted hen's blood—a drop of which down a victim's throat would render him half-paralyzed, lurching about in a synthetic rigor mortis state like a dead man reanimated. Vail rolled up his pack and tucked it away in his sling bag over his shoulder.

When they were finished, they stood in the bedroom and gazed upon the ocean through the back window. It was time for a final goodbye to the house in which the Rane family had lived for generations. Vail and Hondo exchanged a long look, one in which the barbarian saw, for perhaps the first time ever, a sense of sadness in the old man's face. Then Vail climbed onto Hondo's back and strapped himself in for safety. He was too old and frail to rappel down the stone wall alone.

Hondo tied a knot around the wooden post supporting the ceiling in the middle of the bedroom and heaved the heavy rope out the window. He let them down slowly over the edge, climbing down the rope hand under hand and using the flat wall to stabilize themselves with his feet. Madness, the raven, descended alongside, its shadow on the wall beside them cutting the reflection of the moon out over the bay.

A hundred feet down, Hondo transferred his weight to the small ledge jutting out against the jagged rock. The next portion of the down-climb would be more dangerous. Though the wall offered plenty of holds and crimps, they would be without the aid of a rope. Slippery stone evaded a strong purchase; twice they were held only by toe-holds. But they soon cleared the worst of it, making it safely to ground level on the path beside the building.

Vail unclipped himself. Silently, they circumvented the giant stone buildings, crossing the road to the stable where Vail's horse, Stranger, was kept. If Morlon's men were stationed in front of the Rane home, they would not see them down in the road, shielded by buildings.

They retrieved Stranger and started out, the *clip-clop* of hooves echoing through the empty streets. Everywhere garbage drifted aimlessly with the gentle wind. Rats the size of a child's arm dragged streamers, cloth napkins, and chicken bones into their holes.

Continuing without incident, they took side streets and alleys and cut back onto the main road near the edge of the city. There was only one main road in or out of Tarkagen. They proceeded on, glimpsing the outer reaches of the woods ahead when Stranger abruptly stopped. The horse was staring ahead at the forest, but seemed to comprehend none of it.

Vail nudged her with his foot. Stranger stepped forward, then inexplicably reared, whinnying loudly.

Something had her spooked.

The beast would not move.

Hondo squinted at the horizon. "Look."

At first, Vail did not see it. There was only the dim outline of the trees, lit from behind by the silver moonlight, and the clouds on the horizon that diffused the light and . . .

No. It couldn't be.

Vail gasped at the thought. It was too absurd.

Hondo stepped in front of the horse and reached out.

And *tap, tap, tapped* on the wooden facade.

Vail climbed down as well and rapped on the gigantic painted picture of the dim forest. His hand brushed the fake path leading out of the city, to the copse of trees ahead. But it was just a wooden board. It was an illusion.

The wooden facade stretched across the road, a hundred feet across and fifty feet tall, buttressed on either side by the massive stone walls. Hondo pressed against it with both hands; it had no sway. He could not budge it.

They were trapped.

They turned, and a flurry of feet scampered on the bricks around them. In a flash, no less than one hundred men surrounded the two escapees from an elevated position, bows and arrows drawn and ready to pierce their hearts.

Morlon Banchek stood on the parapet above them, shrouded archers bearing emblems of the city stationed on his either side.

A long moment passed. Finally, Morlon did them the courtesy of opening the negotiations. "The emperor requests the elixir, Hondo Rane. He has instructed me to let you live, if you hand it over now."

"What would the emperor have of us," Vail asked, "if we are allowed to live?"

Taking the wizard's question as the opening to a parley, Morlon walked slowly down the stairs. "What does it matter? You'll live. That's more than what I would have in store for you."

Hondo and Vail met eyes. They were smart enough to know that there was no use arguing or pleading their way out of this. There was also no hope of Vail concocting some quick potion with which to bewitch the grunting soldiers.

No, they could only get out of this the old-fashioned way.

"Your facade is well constructed." Hondo tapped again on the false backdrop.

"We wheel it out nightly." Morlon now stood on level ground. Two archers wearing deep-red masks flanked him. "It helps keep a sense of calm and peace in the city."

"The illusion," Hondo responded, "of calm and peace."

Morlon's face was stony. "Illusion, reality, the mind cannot tell the difference."

"The mind knows no lies, then?"

"As long as an illusion elicits the proper reaction, what does it matter? Besides, what lies out there, in the unknowable world, that we cannot provide here? What is so great about fighting to survive—out there?"

"The reality of death is unbeatable," Hondo said. "Your emperor can feign strength in the eyes of the city, but upstairs in his tower, he is dying. All your herbs cannot stem the tide of the undeniable fact that all men die—and die alone.

"So now you must have this." Hondo pulled the glass vial from his cloak pocket and held it up. The archers' bows wobbled slightly; they could taste their prize.

Hondo uncapped the vial. Tendrils of vapor rose. He held it straight out, threatening to upend it. The crowd gasped.

"No!" Morlon held up his palms and dropped to his knees. Fear flashed in his eyes. "For the love of Chamath, don't! You can leave freely, but do not waste the elixir." He stood shakily, staggering closer. "Hand it over and you can go. You can live. Please."

"If you want it," Hondo said, "then you will grant me one request."

"What is it?" Morlon fidgeted with his cane.

"Fight me."

Morlon looked around at his one hundred men.

"Have your men put down your bows," Hondo said. "And battle me in the street. If you can take me down, you can take the vial."

He watched Morlon's face as the captain contemplated. Morlon had one hundred men. The odds of him losing were almost nil. And the emperor would gladly give every man's life to have the elixir. No price was too high. Hondo knew Morlon was aware of this. He could only hope that the captain would not see fit to dishonor his old friend by calling on his archers to fill him full of arrows, thus calling his bluff. For the potion itself could never be destroyed; if poured on the ground it would not dissolve. Only a human had the power to digest it. And that must never happen.

Morlon made his decision. With a wave of his finger, he signaled his men. One by one they set their bows and arrows down. Their metal legs clanked in unison as they marched down the steps. Each withdrew a sword from the sheath on his back.

The soldiers stood there, masked and ready, opposite this beast with piston arms and fanged teeth. The barbarian let his cloak fall and pulled out his sword. Gasping as the giant's bulky frame was revealed, they swallowed hard and prepared for battle.

Then it was on.

Chapter 9

Hondo had learned of his father's death while on crusade against the Mujeel army. Word had been given to him by the wiry messenger with the fox fur around his neck. It had been bitterly cold on the plains, the two opposing armies stomping their feet for warmth. The battle was just about to begin.

Upon hearing the news, Hondo felt nothing. The man who had simultaneously taught and tormented him was dead and gone, and he felt nothing. Hondo would not be going back for the burial. His duty was here on the battlefield, and it was not custom for giants to break battle, not even for loved ones.

The great significance of his trials with his father would not be realized for many years, not until the fight of his life, which was about to begin.

The soldiers clashed with Hondo in a volley of swings and thrusts. Steel flinted and men screamed and swore, and some gasped before sputtering into gurgles of froth. One after the other, they came to blows with the warrior. Some were impaled, others picked up and thrown by Hondo headfirst into stone, splintering their spines into chips. One skittish soldier watched in horror as Hondo sank his fangs into his cousin's neck. Hondo emerged from the spurting red fountain, bits of flesh in his mouth, a naked, demonic grin across his face as he chewed and swallowed the skin.

The bashing continued. Legs, split from their owners, shuddered for precious few seconds before the nerves in them rested. One soldier was stabbed up the arse, the steel protruding from the center of his chest. No man should be able to remove such a deep blade like that from a human, but Hondo could, and did, with ease.

Morlon Banchek watched calmly from his place on the stairs, as his soldiers screamed and flailed impotently against the blows of the barbarian. Hondo showed no signs of slowing, the blood and entrails strewn on the stone only fueling his rage and imbuing him with a divine power and madness. This was his territory, his expertise. None of these fighters had seen anything like war as Hondo had. They lacked the drive, the intensity, the swordsmanship. Hondo felt invincible. Send them all, he thought, send all the emperor's soldiers, and I shall ravage each as cleanly as the last. Blood sprayed. Men were delimbed. Hondo shrieked with delight.

He leapt upon a lone soldier and hooked a thumb in his nostril, ripping a hunk of nose away, cartilage bursting and tearing from the man's face. As Hondo spun around to face another dozen soldiers approaching from the front, Morlon made his move.

Between his splayed fingers, in each hand, he held three small mirrors. He walked behind the giant and held them up as Hondo turned and caught sight of himself.

Everything abruptly stopped. A strange silence stole over him. He gripped his sword but did not swing it. He went wide-eyed as the illusion in the glass began to work on him. Mesmerized, he could only watch. He saw nothing except the moving picture that had formed. The images joined as one, and the battle and soldiers around him faded away until only the illusion remained.

The man in the mirror—Hondo—grew younger and younger. It was the same trick he had seen upon entering the city, but this time the illusion was more powerful and pronounced. He simply could not tear himself away. Inside the mirror, he watched himself. Soon he was a small boy, not even ten years old.

Little Hondo stood alone in his old room, sobbing, staring at the floor. Someone was chastising him. The child looked up as a loud voice broke into the silent vision. And as the illusion grew in intensity, Hondo Rane found himself merging with the image completely, until he was the ten-year-old boy staring up at his father, Thursday Rane, who glared at him, screaming and full of fury.

His father appeared clear as day. He wore the wide brown belt made of buckskin, the feeling of which Hondo knew well on his backside. The man's countenance was hard, stern, unforgiving, never a smile to be offered. Dark eyes and heavy eyebrows furrowed in constant agitation. The rage exacerbated by the alcohol. The hands —the soft hands of a civilized man that took their frustration out on the young Hondo.

His father bellowed incoherently. Little Hondo didn't know what the argument was about, and it didn't matter much. Thursday Rane had never loved his son— and if he did, that love was smothered by the blankets of shame and inadequacy at having had to raise a barbarian.

Now he grabbed Hondo. Soon the boy's face pressed hard against the stone wall, his wrists chained. The blows came. He felt the flesh of his back splitting in jagged tears.

Back in battle, Hondo Rane sank to his knees and whimpered with each blow to his childhood self.

And the blows came down, in battle, though Hondo's mind was in the past. Morlon signaled for the soldiers to whip the poor giant into exhaustion. He wanted the barbarian alive; he would be greatly rewarded for the retrieval of the vial and the man who deigned to escape with it.

With each crack of the whip, Hondo's panic grew. One lash caught his left eye, taking him to his knees. It split him at the pupil, coming in razor-hot. Jelly spilled down his cheek. The vision in that eye went full dark in an instant.

Welts, wet and ugly, sprang up. Blow after blow rained down, and with each one he heard a voice, not outside, but from inside his own head. Their whips were indistinguishable from his father's. His father's hand, their hands, intermingled with cursing and the stink of alcohol. His father, who tried so hard to beat the barbarian out of him—who cursed the ancient line in his own blood that produced such a son. In both worlds, Hondo's arms were raised; in the past, they were chained to the stone. In the present, he held them up himself, unaware he could let them down at any time—if only he could see the truth.

And through all this, Vail did not interfere. He simply watched from his horse, waiting for the right moment to act.

Morlon, meanwhile, saw Hondo transfix upon the images in his own brain. In glee, he watched the inner thoughts reflected in the barbarian's eyes. He shuddered with pleasure in his front row view to the child's pain.

In his vision, Hondo grew weak. His arms went slack as he sank to his knees. Chains tore his wrists. He closed his eyes. He wanted it to be over; no more, no more. To end this soon would be a pleasure.

Then, the impact of the blows began to recede into the background of his mind. They became fainter, duller.

The inchoate screaming of his father dimmed as well.

He heard a voice reaching for him, somewhere deep inside the dream, inside himself. Something called. Slowly, he lifted his head. The image of his father grew hazy, and split apart. The pieces drifted away and faded from view. The beatings. The teasing from other boys. His brother, Garson, who never came to his aid, avoiding his glares. Soon he was left with only the raw emotions of never living up to the expectations of the civilized world.

In the present, Hondo's vision went blank. All sensation left him. There was only the blankness of white in front of him. And Vail, sitting there, calmly, cross-legged, mystically, watching him.

Though Vail's mouth did not move, the voice came through softly, gently.

Do you remember what I told you the day you left home?

Hondo stared at the old wizard. He struggled to remember.

Think, Hondo. Remember.

Hondo furrowed his brow. *You told me I was a warrior.*

I did. Now tell me this. Do you want to survive?

Yes.

Why? Why do you want to live?

Because . . . because . . .

Because you fight?

Yes!

Why do you fight?

I'm a barbarian.

Do you believe that? With all your heart?

Yes!

Then, Hondo, why do you pine for something other than what you are? If you are a barbarian, why do you shame yourself with these memories? Why do you indulge them?

Hondo had no answer.

This man, Morlon, is about to capture you, enslave you forever. The elixir will be lost. He has you wrapped in a delusion. Unless you break it, all is lost. I cannot do it for you. You must do it alone.

He has power over me.

Yes. Your shame gives him power. Your shame is the gateway to the delusion, Hondo. It is a lie. You must let it go.

My father fought who I was.

Yes.

My brother fought who I was.

Yes. And there is one place you have not looked for the answers. It is only there that you will find a way out of this.

Hondo thought. The sounds of the men in battle, and of his father, hummed in the background of his consciousness.

From behind Vail stepped the young boy. Hondo the young one. And old Hondo gazed upon his younger self —and saw himself.

And he felt a surge of love well up in his heart for himself, for the boy who bore the terrible burden of being born. He wanted to cry out to him, to tell him what he knew now that he did not know then, that there was no shame in it, there was no shame in being alive.

I see. I see it now.

Yes, Hondo. I know that you do.

The boy could not be something other than what he was. To survive now, I must . . . yes, I understand. I see it now!

Then rise, Hondo the Horrible. Protect the boy.

Protect myself. Yes. I see it now.

Break the spell. Show them. Show them who you are.

Hondo knew as he opened his eyes. He felt himself being pulled out of the mirrors, and then he was standing there, looking at Morlon Banchek's twisted smile. The whips befalling him bore him no pain.

He simply stood and let the beatings continue. Slowly a grin grew, and then a deep, booming laugh exploded from his belly. With one swift move, his hand found the next whip poised to strike him. He grabbed it—and pulled!—and flung the man holding it head over arse. The soldier's back broke as he slammed against the heavy wooden facade.

The strength of the beast gave the others pause. The smile fell from Morlon's face as Hondo spoke.

"Illusions make men weak, Banchek," Hondo said. "They make feeble your mind and body. I know, because I saw it. I lived it. I was at the mercy of the delusions of others until I left home.

"But reality creates strong men. And I was born in the world. *The real world.* I have lived there all my life. I am strong because I live in the world of blood and glory and battle. I am built to fight corrupt kings and monsters alike. There is no one like me in this world.

"My name is Hondo Rane. I am powerful. I am a warrior. *I am a barbarian.*"

Quick as a cat's leap, Hondo swung his sword and cleaved Banchek down the middle, from head to groin. His blade cleanly split the man in two. The halves of the corpse fell limply to the ground, an outstretched look of shock on both parts of the man's face.

Roaring, he plowed his way through the remaining men. Stomping ahead, he arched his sword right to left, and let go, taking their heads clean off. He felt each soul leaving the body. Instinct took over amid the flow of the battle. The gods were with him. He could sense their cheering from the rafters of heaven. They were his true family. They and Vail, and that was all he needed.

Soon the battle was soon over. There was no one left to kill. Hondo had won.

Vail stood and clapped a hand on Hondo's shoulder as if to say, "Good work."

Bits of yellow light were streaming down now. As if on cue, the gate began to slide open. It was daytime and the city was opening. The wooden facade gave way to the real path to the real forest.

Vail mounted Stranger. They left the city. There was still a long way to go. Though they'd passed their first serious test, there would be many more on their flight to safety. Any moment now, the emperor would learn of his defeat and send his army after them; they'd need to reach their destination quickly and regroup.

But for now, they were free.

And for Hondo, in more ways than one.

Dogfight

"This isn't real!" Elliot screamed over the flight helmet microphone. He yanked the control stick and began the defensive split; soon he and his wingman in the fighter jet behind him would be far enough apart for proper maneuvers. As they splintered out of formation, he could see the enemy's yellow tracers shooting past his window and streaking across the deep blue sky.

"Don't say that!" Dylan Reynolds yelled. "It doesn't help! Shit!" Their comms crackled.

Elliot blinked hard. *Stay here, stay here now,* he told himself. *This* is *real. Don't fight it. It'll only make things worse.*

Regaining his breathing, talking himself down, he made it real. *You and your best friend are being chased by a Terran fighter jet. You're in the North Pacific, almost to Old Japan. You're a commander, damn it. Now act like one!*

"Okay." He took a deep breath and steadied the control stick with both hands. "I'm going to break left. You do just as we practiced, got it?"

"Yes, sir."

"One, two, mark!"

Elliot dove left as his wingman braked hard and pulled up. He felt the familiar sinking in his gut as he angled himself down, down, down, and entered a barrel roll, the enemy's tracers so close now he could almost smell them scorching the sky.

"Dylan!" The rapid beep-beep-beep in his ear made his breath catch and heart freeze. The enemy had him in his sights. "He's got me on lock! I can't shake him! I can't shake him!"

He closed his eyes, waiting for the shock blast. In his last brief moment he said goodbye to his friends and family and went deep inside himself, bracing for impact. But the shock wave he felt was not from his plane exploding.

In disbelief, he watched as the gray jet of his partner blew past him, carrying fragments of the destroyed fighter in his wake.

"Whoo! Got him!" Dylan's cheers rang through his headset. "Just in the nick of time!"

Elliot let out a shuddery breath as the adrenaline dissipated. In their flights so far, the enemy had never locked on him, never gotten that close to taking him out. Nausea rolled over him—ecstasy, hopelessness, every emotion all at once as his body tried to recover. The last time he felt this bad was when he got the draft card coming home from school telling him he'd been chosen to fly. The difference was he'd been able to sit at the kitchen table to gather himself and calm his nerves. But there was no time for that now. He had a job to do—bombs to drop—and even less time now to do it in.

"Roger that," he said. "Nice work. Bring it in close."

A few seconds later they were flying side by side. Elliot flashed him a thumbs-up through the window. "Only eight minutes out." He flicked a switch. "Let's start prepping the load."

"Copy that."

They flew on, passing not a single cloud. Back home in Ohio, the weather had always been so gray it made him feel as though he were imprisoned by clouds. But out here, a young man like him could truly feel free. He let himself enjoy the sight for another minute before checking in. "Getting any readings, Reynolds?"

The voice in the headset crackled. "Negative, sir."

"Stay icy. I don't want any surprises. Not this late in the game."

"Yes, sir."

Elliot winced. "And don't call me—" He cut himself off.

"You say something, sir?"

"No. Never mind."

"You're a corporal now." Elliot could hear him grinning. "Friends or not, I gotta call you sir."

"Fine." Elliot grunted and checked his instruments. They were close now—real close. Just three minutes away. Their plan was simple: reach their target, drop their load, and hightail it back to base. Fortunately, he saw no enemy fighters on radar.

Two minutes out.

"Okay, Reynolds, I'm opening the hatch." Elliot twisted a knob and heard the whirring of the gears. Air whizzing by at two thousand miles per hour rattled the hydrogen bombs in their stronghold. "Cover me. Attack formation."

One minute out.

"Sir?" Reynolds's voice, timid.

"What is it?"

"Something's up with my radar, sir."

"What's wrong?" Elliot held his breath, gathering his strength as a commander. "I said, what's wrong, Private!"

"I-I'm not sure yet."

"You're scared, Private."

"I'm terrified, sir. Something's really w-wrong."

"Reynolds, hold it together, you hear me—"

Beep. Beep. Beep.

"Oh, God." Reynolds's voice cracked. "You hear that, Elliot? They're closing in."

Beep. Beep. Beep.

Elliot craned his neck. "All I see are clouds, Private. Do you have a visual?" He tapped on his radar, seeing nothing.

"They're not on radar! Why aren't they on radar?"

"Calm down, Private!"

Elliot checked again. Nothing but blue sky and yellow sun.

"Sir, I—"

"Quiet, Dylan. We drop in t-minus twenty seconds. No excuses, you hear me? Say 'affirmative, sir.'"

"A-a-affirmative, sir."

Beep beep beep beep beep beep—

This isn't real, this isn't real, this isn't really real this isn't—

The realization hit Elliot like a bullet. "They're Mirrors!" Elliot screamed into his mic. "They're below us! Evasive maneuvers, now!"

As he let the bombs loose, Elliot swung left and entered his half-loop. The enemy jet fired its weapons from below, missing his plane by mere yards and whistling past him. Breaking back right, Elliot maneuvered into a barrel roll, swung his nose dead-on, and fired. The enemy jet exploded like a bag of glitter.

But there was a second explosion as well, and he watched his friend's plane incinerate in the hot summer sky. The Terran fighter had gotten off one shot before the explosion, and that's all it needed.

Elliot began to cry as the steely voice of his commander crackled over his headset. "Bring it in, Corporal," it said.

He disconnected his mask and stifled his cries. "D-Dylan," he blubbered.

The reply was soft. "Bring it in, Corporal. That's an order."

The dome opened and Elliot, dressed in his Company Games uniform, stepped out and stood at the front of his cubicle. He wiped his nose with the back of his hand. He didn't want to look, but did anyway as two cubicles over, the marshals were already wrenching the screaming Dylan from his simulation chair.

The last thing he saw was Dylan's outstretched fingers as they slipped through Death's Door.

The soldier countdown above the door dropped from

64 / 100 to 63 / 100.

Vincent stepped up beside him, munching a protein bar and wearing a damp towel around his neck.

"Sucks about Dylan, man. But at least you got the mission done. Woulda been both of you going through Death's Door otherwise." He swallowed. "Those Mirrors are real sonsabitches, huh? Refracting light like that, staying off your radar. It's all part of the game getting harder now."

He tossed his wrapper in the trash. "I gotta get back. My next simulation starts soon. Once we hit sixty men left, the break between runs drops to five minutes. Well, see ya." He disappeared from the kitchen.

Elliot checked the clock. 3:04 a.m. He'd been flying for his life for twenty-two hours straight.

He walked to the kitchen and shakily poured a cup of coffee.

In the next room over, the bank of commentators began their next transmission. Over one billion people were eagerly waiting for updates on the most dangerous video game competition in the world.

He glanced up at the television in the corner. The news was already reporting the death of his best friend, Dylan, as he was disposed of on the other side of Death's Door.

Die in simulation, the draft letter had read, *die in the real world. But survive Dogfight, and win* 5,000,000 *credits.* A fortune, all right, enough to buy anything a young man could ever want.

With trembling hands he sipped his coffee, pushing away thoughts of his mother, who had wept when he was called up, and Dylan Reynolds, and his other friends who were relieved they hadn't been drafted, but who snubbed him all the same after learning he'd been chosen. Easier to ignore the person who might die than deal with the difficult feelings of saying goodbye.

He shook his head. This was no time to mourn. He had to focus up.

3:10 a.m.

One of the referees stuck his head in. "Time to saddle up, Elliot. Take off in two minutes."

He nodded and drained the rest of his coffee. He'd need as much as he could get.

He stood, left the kitchen, and entered his dome. The lid closed with a pneumatic thunk.

This isn't real, he told himself. *This isn't real.*

But Dylan had been right, he realized as the screen came up. He shouldn't say that anymore.

It didn't help.

It didn't help at all.

I'm Ready to Affirm
You Now, Gamma

ROUND THE TIME THE COUNTRY WAS SWERVING headlong into mental illness, Richard Kaye was standing outside the terminal, smoking a cigarette, watching the robo-planes whizzing to and from the New Las Vegas airport.

He exhaled the last bit of smoke and tossed the butt. Almost twenty-eight credits for dirt tobacco, he thought bitterly. What is the world coming to?

Hoisting his duffel bag, he poked through the sidewalks of people gathering around the autonomous taxis like frothy swarms of bees. He entered the airport and located his wife, Shelley, who was holding their spot in the security checkpoint line with their twin boys, Oscar and Dede, both seven.

They'd arrived eight hours early, which was customary in those days.

The line for the Alpha-Omega Airlines terminal was already a quarter-mile long. Keeping everyone company were the screens blasting at full volume that stretched along the walls on either side.

Richard handed his family their ear plugs. The telescreens could not be turned down. He'd asked five employees, but none of them knew how to do it.

"Today, August 8, 2049, it's The News!" A newscaster screamed.

Two hours later, the line had moved twelve feet. Since Affirmation had become a standard practice, the lines always went slowly, although One-State claimed Affirmation always helped them go faster.

Three hours later, they were almost to the front of the line. Richard fidgeted.

Seeing what awaited them made him nervous.

He cursed under his breath. They never should have come. This was a mistake. This whole idea of taking the family to Hawaii for two weeks, their first real vacation since the twins were born, had been a colossal misjudgment.

But there was no going back. He knew it. So did Shelley. She could tell what he was thinking. She pulled him along.

The vacation was really happening then. This was really happening. After two years of planning, they were going.

But first, they had to be Affirmed.

AT THE CHECKPOINT, THE LINE SPLIT INTO SEVERAL. Shelley took the twins to the Thetas and Zetas line. Thetas used to correspond to something, Zetas to something else. The Alliance of Affirmation decreed that anyone could be a Theta and anyone a Zeta. Anyone could be any of the seventeen options listed, in fact. No one knew the difference between them. But everyone had to choose.

The listless military man at the booth separating the lines chewed his gum. "Boarding pass, ID, Social Security card, immigration reports . . ."

Richard handed everything over.

"Mother's maiden name?" the agent said.

"Moore," Richard said.

"Name of third grade teacher?" the agent said.

"Dr. Russo," Richard said.

"Father's weight?" the agent said.

This went on for some time, until the agent and the dragonfly drones above were satisfied.

"You understand that all medical tests will be done to you at the sole discretion of One-State?"

Richard swallowed. "Yes."

"You affirm your loyalty to One-State and to the patriotic duty known as Affirmation? I can explain this in greater detail for you."

"No, thank you." Richard's mouth felt like sandpaper. "I understand."

He glanced at the Theta and Zeta line. Shelley and the kids were being given the same speech. The children were on their tablets, thank God. In fact, all the children in line were on their tablets. That was good. Distraction was good. Behind his family was a young Theta or Zeta running their finger on the on-screen penguin, tracking the outline of its body and filling in the belly with red paint. When Theta or Zeta ran their finger out of the line, the penguin's face curled up and its mouth foamed with rage. Sometimes it screamed, the haptic signals in the device sending a small shock and causing Theta or Zeta to drop the tablet. He watched the Theta or Zeta parent exhale loudly and scold her little Theta or Zeta and threaten them with a grounding if the tablet broke.

The military agent handed Richard back his documents.

"As a One-State ambassador," he said," I want to affirm your Decency and Humanity." He put his hands together and offered the bow made customary by the One-State Inclusion and Affirmation For All Act of 2044.

"Thank you," Richard said. His whole body felt slippery. There was a puddle in his shoes.

"How do you prefer to be Affirmed today, sir? You can choose Theta, Zeta, Lambda, Iota . . ." He listed off several options.

"I—I don't know.

"We can Affirm you any way you want."

"Please call me Richard."

"You must choose one of the options," the agent repeated.

"I want to be Affirmed as Richard."

The agent exhaled loudly. His annoyance seemed to cause him physical pain. "That is not one of our choices. How about Gamma?"

When he didn't respond fast enough, the agent simply yanked Richard by the elbow to the Gamma line, which was exactly the same as the other lines. His belongings were unceremoniously dumped from his suitcase onto the table.

A drone buzzed next to his head. "Step through the scanner, please."

Richard stepped through the millimeter wave scanner. Agents behind the machine studied something.

"This way," the drone said. "Into the x-ray machine."

Gulping, Richard entered the dark station and waited for the buzz to indicate the x-ray had been taken. Exiting, he stopped between the white lines on the floor that demarcated the noninvasive checking station.

Twenty-nine minutes later, a corpulent Theta or Zeta appeared. The Theta or Zeta snapped their gloves and said: "To protect the safety of yourself and other passengers, I'm going to Affirm you now. You are a beautiful Theta or Zeta, and I want to Affirm your Decency. Do you go by Theta or Zeta?"

Richard stammered.

The Theta or Zeta checked their notes. "My sincerest apologies, Gamma. I did not mean to call you that."

"Please call me Richard."

"Okay, Gamma. Are you ready to be Seen and Affirmed? Your Decency is very important to us."

"I—well—"

"Would you like to be Affirmed in the front hole or the back hole?"

Richard's stomach leapt high into his throat. "Back hole," he found himself croaking.

"Please face the wall."

Richard did.

"Please slide your pants down."

He unbuttoned his pants, unzipped his fly, and let his pants fall. His hands shook.

The masked attendant slid Richard's underwear to his ankles.

"Are you ready, Gamma?"

"Please call me Richard."

"Under the One-State Inclusion and Affirmation For All Act of 2044—"

"Never mind, just hurry, for the love of God—"

"Maybe Mr. Gamma? Mrs. Gamma? Gamma Gamma?"

Silence.

"I'm happy to See and Affirm you in any way you'd like."

"Richard. Call me Richard."

"I'm going to Affirm you now, Gamma," the attendant said.

He spread Richard's butt cheeks with one hand and slipped the other into the vat of Affirmation Jelly on the floor. Jammed his index finger inside and wiggled it about until the jelly was thick.

He stuck his slimy finger into Richard's back hole and felt around. Richard squirmed.

When the attendant was satisfied, he removed his finger.

"Wait here, Gamma." The masked attendant stepped to the assay machine to his right and smeared the nasty remnants onto the glass dish. The machine sucked the glass plate into its interior. It burped as if digesting a meal.

The light on it turned yellow.

The masked attendant gathered his report and returned to Richard. "Sir, have you ever been diagnosed with an intestinal disorder?"

"No."

"Hmm. Interesting. The report came back inconclusive. We'll have to Affirm you again."

A few minutes later a second agent approached, snapping his gloves. "How would you like to be Seen today?"

Richard stared blankly.

"There are seventeen ways I can See you," the agent said, holding up a laminated 8"x11" card bearing all the ways one can be Seen. There were Zeta, Theta, Gamma, of course, and many others. Next to each Way of Being Seen was an illustration of a stick figure with slight variations. Every month or so, the illustrations would change. The illustrations were so simple a child could pick one.

After twelve minutes of explaining each Way of Being Seen, the agent checked his notes, apologizing for not seeing that Richard had already been labeled Gamma. He proceeded to gather a specimen, this time from much deeper inside Richard, and had to ask for help to pry open Richard's back hole.

When it was over, Richard trembled and pulled up his pants. Two of the nearby floor drones cackled as they rifled through his clothes that had slipped off the counter.

The machine dinged. Its light turned yellow.

"I'm sorry, Gamma," the agent said, "The reports are inconclusive. We'll have to Affirm you again."

Richard slumped, his face dropping. At once he looked a hundred years old. He tried to fathom what he'd just heard. Another Affirmation? His eyes were vacant as the agent turned away to prepare a third round of Affirmation Jelly.

"Again?"

"Yes, Gamma, once more."

Richard glanced past the Affirmation Station. His family stood just beyond the machines, all three having completed and passed their Affirmations. Shelley waved. Oscar waved. Dede waved. All grinning. Ready. Ready for vacation.

Waiting.

Waiting for him.

His vision went flat. How could they, his own family, look happy? How could everyone else, all these people, be okay with all this? Wasn't there something horribly wrong? Did anyone else see it? Was he the only one?

Or was he all alone?

"Gamma," the agent said. "Follow me to your next Affirmation."

The lights burned his eyes. Dragonfly drones gathered above. All of them were filming and taking scans and measurements of serotonin, dopamine, temperature readings.

"Gamma? Come with me now!"

Everyone and everything seemed so far away. The smiles of his wife and children had disappeared. He saw only their impending horror at what would happen if he refused.

Richard willed himself to move. Tried with all his power, all the determination he could muster, but his legs did not respond. His eyes were dazed and glassy. He wanted to speak. Could only shake his head.

And the red and yellow lights above were whirling and screeching and the drones were buzzing, and now more guards appeared, sizzle sticks at their side, edging toward him as if he were a rabid mutt.

Richard look around, but there was nowhere to run.

The entire crowd was watching now. Shelley had her arms raised, yelling at him.

Oscar was yelling, too. So was Dede.

"Do it, Dad!" they said. "Let them do it!"

"Bend over!" Shelley screamed. "Just let them do it already!"

He looked over the faces of his family.

They saw nothing wrong with this.

No one did.

It was he who must be crazy. Not them.

He thought of their anger, their disappointment with him if they missed their vacation.

The guards raised their sizzle sticks and drew closer. Soon they would shock him.

There was no way out.

He could not resist.

They had won.

Upon accepting this truth, he felt something tear in his psyche.

When the pressure in his head and chest was gone for good, so was Richard.

Slouching, his face contorted in cognitive agony, Gamma Kaye followed the agent to his next Affirmation.

Seeds

Devon was dreaming when the wah-wah alert on his phone yanked him from his sleep.

"Devon." The voice on the other end whispered.

He sat up. "Doctor Eiseley?" And when no answer came, he knew what was happening. "You found it. Didn't you?"

The response took a long time.

"Yes, I've . . . yes. I believe so."

"How? What was the compound, what was the process—"

"It's best if you see for yourself."

"But sir—"

"Just come."

"Yessir, I'm coming now, let me get dressed! Doctor?

Doctor!"

He spoke to an empty line.

Fifteen minutes later, Devon stood on the brakes before nearly crashing the gate at Belmont Labs. He'd not taken his foot off the gas the whole drive over, roaring over the concrete sprawl of Livermore, California.

The robotic guard scanned his eye and let him through the gate. He gunned the car again and skidded to a stop at the two-story building in the back of the lot and unlocked the door. An adrenaline-fueled sprint propelled him to the fourth-floor lab where he'd worked for the last five years.

Loren Eiseley was peering out the window. He seemed oddly calm for a man who'd just made the greatest discovery of all time, his arms resting behind his back like that.

He turned to Devon. As always, he wore a suit and tie and his round glasses with wire frames. He smiled thinly and faced the window again, though he wasn't watching the parking lot. He was gazing at the field that lay beyond.

Devon pointed to the table, at the lone microscope and the petri dish below its lens. "Is this it?" Without waiting for an answer, he unwrapped his scarf from around his neck and flung it on the chair. Sitting down, he saw, and gasped.

"Cellular activity in the protein!"

"Yes."

"Sir, you've done it. You've actually done it!"

Silence.

Devon stood. "You've got to be excited. You've created

life! From nothing! This is—this is—"

"Big."

"Yes!" Devon's mind raced at this culmination of their work together. "Organic matter from inorganic compounds. You've mixed the ingredients together and unlocked the secret of the universe." His eyes glazed over. "The secret of life itself."

"No, my young friend. We haven't."

"But we have, sir, it's right here. *It's all right here.* Before your eyes. It's alchemy. It's—impossible, but we've discovered what creates life!"

"Life has made itself. We've discovered nothing."

Devon was speechless. He shook his head and set his hands on his hips. "Sir, I don't understand."

Eiseley sighed and rubbed his head. His sixty-three-year crusade for the secret of life lay in a petri dish, and he was tired.

"Doctor," Devon said, "here you are with the find of a thousand years—hell, fourteen billion years—the discovery of the life protein, which converts inorganic material into living mass—and you look like you were just diagnosed as terminal. Have you forgotten why we've been studying all this time, searching for answers together? To solve the mystery of life is to defeat humanity's greatest enemy: Death!"

Eiseley turned. "Yes. Life itself. The secret of all animate life on the planet. We've forced nature to prostitute herself to us! Right here, in this lab! We've bent her to our will, and now her secrets are ours. You and I, funded by One-State, who set us up here so we could rip nature up from the ground and take it all."

He continued. "I can see your look. You think I'm being too harsh. That I'm unfair. Well, I'm only telling the truth. You and I have lied to ourselves for too long. We've hidden behind our love for science. By discovering this protein, we've potentially destroyed the sanctity of life."

"Sir, what do you mean 'the sanctity of life'? This discovery will help *every human on the planet.* This could be the key to stopping illness, to replenishing ecosystems, to ending the process of aging. Why, we could live forever! Who knows what the implications of finding the life protein could be."

Eiseley gazed wistfully out the window. "I already know the implications, the potential . . . and the doom this will bring on the world."

"Doom, sir?"

"Although it seems like we've found something spectacular, by creating animate life from inanimate life, all we've done is open a *new* rabbit hole. No, we are further from cracking the cosmic egg of life than ever before."

"But you have the *formula!*" Devon's voice cracked. He strained to understand his mentor's point. "You have the compound, the proportions, the temperature, the blueprint of life—you have *everything!*"

"We don't know everything. We know the blueprint of the blueprint, the combination of materials and how they scrape against other materials and so forth, and the alternating heat and cold they require. Oh, yes, but those are simply the materials of the body, and not of the spirit.

"Don't you see, this is no different from understanding how babies are made. We can create children, yes? Sperm and egg, of course, and yet—*and yet* —we do not understand *how* life really starts—and for what purpose.

"Think about it. If we rewind all of the history of life on this planet, back down to our own primordial ooze of the swamp, back to the basic particles of the atom—and farther!—what of the proteins that comprise the proteins? What created the universe? *What of life itself?*"

Devon thought for a moment. This was something to consider. Still: "I disagree."

"You do?"

"Yes. You've done something all of the scientific community has been trying to achieve since Darwin. You've gone farther down the ladder of evolution than anyone. If you want to deny that, you go ahead. But don't expect me to follow."

Eiseley was silent for a long time. "We are further from the truth of life than ever before. We still don't have the *essence* of life, and I don't believe it's possible to have it. We've created life in a lab, but we don't know what animated it. So what if the conditions are two parts hydrogen, five parts carbon, a pinch of oxygen, a dash of that? The parts and temperatures and all the rest does not explain the *process* of what gave *life* to the protein, or how it became a protein in the first place!

"We have to be very careful now. We know what will happen if One-State finds our work. They'll proclaim its success to the world, make a big show so the President and his cronies can take credit for it. Our knowledge will not be used for good. They'll use it for war and death, not for life. They'll produce weapons, or men who can never die, or rocks that turn into robots. It will be used to control life, not create it.

"Men with cameras will take over our lives. You and I will be made famous, and make millions."

"Sounds pretty good, if you ask me."

Eiseley frowned. "And our work, and the cause for which we work? The cause of science? Of life? One-State will say that life starts and stops with matter—that they alone possess the tools to create and destroy—and it will all be a lie."

"Then what do you suggest we do? What's the point of our time together, if you're just going to throw it all away?"

Eiseley gestured broadly to the lone field that lay beyond the concrete walls and barbed wire fences surrounding the lab.

"When I was younger," he said, "I would hop the fence into the yard behind my house and walk for hours, days, weeks. Who knows how long. I'd lose track of time, wandering in the tall grass, returning home only when I felt like it. I talked to the trees and laughed with the squirrels and spied on the deer. It was so long ago. . .

"When you traipse through the weeds and wild grasses, things cling to you. Leaves, insects—and seeds. The seeds would hug my shoe, my jacket. How? I could never tell. They're not supposed to be intelligent. That's what our scientists say, anyway. But that's how flowers and trees and shrubs move around, by spreading their seeds and taking root in a new place.

"How many One-State scientists do you know who would label that as anything but a survival mechanism, the action of some natural automaton, like a robot, a reflex encoded in the plant to open with the sun? They would never say seeds are smart.

"But they cling. They grasp things! They catch rides and spread themselves over the land. Then they detach, when the time is right, and they grow and blossom and eat and feed other creatures. What *particle* accounts for that decision-making? What *mechanism* caused this step in its evolution? See, that is life, and we'll never find it in a lab!"

Eiseley turned around and shouldered a large backpack. Devon hadn't seen it lying there. Nor had he noticed the boots the professor was wearing.

"Where are you going?" he asked.

"Out." Eiseley snapped the buckle on his pack around his waist and cinched the strap.

"Out where?"

Eiseley nodded toward the window. "Into the field. To search for the secret of life. *The real secret of life.* Back to where I belong, among the seeds and pods and the husks of dead things. I've wasted too much of my time in a lab. And time is short."

"Sir, you can't just leave!"

"You could come with me."

"Where?" Devon said. "Out there?"

"Yes, *out there!*" Eiseley set a hand on the young man's shoulder. "Don't make the same mistake I did. Life, real life, is in the fields, in the sands, in the oceans. One day you'll wake up and all your years will have flashed off, and your work will have been stolen, and you'll have nothing but comfort and security and money, and they will be like a noose around your neck. You'll know everything about chemicals and compositions, but nothing of the song of a whale or the yip of the prairie dog, and you'll wonder what it would have been like to go out there, to walk barefoot on the plains and carry the seeds of the grasslands on your jeans."

He stared at the young man for several moments. But Devon had nothing to say.

Eiseley nodded with finality and shouldered his bag.

"Before you go," Devon said, "please give me the data. You don't have to take credit. I'll be responsible. I'll handle the burden."

Loren smiled gently. "I'm sorry. But I can't."

"Please!" Devon sank to his knees. All his work, about to walk out the door forever. "Give me the name of the protein and measurements of the elements you combined." He clasped his hands. "I'll figure out the temperatures, I don't need anything else. I'm begging you!"

"The data is gone, my friend."

"Gone?" Devon's eyes went wide.

"Destroyed. Poof. Finished."

Devon rushed to the petri dish, as if to save something, anything.

"Only a duplicate of a generic compound," Eiseley said. "You've been a good partner. But please understand. There's nothing here for me, or for you. Not now. Life— *life*—is out *there*. I might even catch a glimpse of it, finally. Can you imagine?" He went to the door.

"I'll tell the guards." Devon threatened. "I'll tell everyone. You haven't destroyed everything. You wouldn't!"

Eiseley turned. "The hard drives are already down the incinerator. If you rush fast enough, you may be able to salvage some of them. Assuming, of course, you can force me to give up my passwords." He checked his watch. "But you only have about thirty seconds until the incinerators run again."

Devon said nothing. He had the look of a man knocked out of the ring.

He listened as Eiseley tromped down the stairwell

whistling a nameless tune. Then he heard the crashing of the outer door, the clang of the lock. He walked back to the window and peered out. His boss appeared below, crossing the lot to the wall and the barbed-wire fence beyond.

Eiseley threw his backpack over and began to scale the fence. Soon he too was over, and after a minute Devon lost sight of him completely. Somewhere in the distance, Devon thought, maybe, there was a glint of moonlight catching something metallic—a belt buckle, perhaps. But it was only a flash, and then his mentor was gone for good, out among the seeds and the pods and the husks of dead things.

Family

ON THE LAMINATE TABLE IN THE CENTER OF THE living room of the one-bedroom apartment sat the vase of plastic daisies and sunflowers that hadn't moved in over nine years. It was never dusted or cleaned, which was how Olivia Abbott wanted it.

Every morning she would exit her bedroom at 6 a.m., walk down the short hallway into the living room, and start her day by sipping coffee and watching the fake flowers move gently as she breathed on them from her seat at the table.

After her caffeine she would stretch before her food arrived promptly at seven. She'd been adamant about this when she signed her lease—all meals were to be delivered at 7 a.m., noon, and 4 p.m.

She liked to read in the mornings too, more than

ever during winter when it was still dark out.

But not today.

Everything was different today.

It had been hard to sleep, that was for sure. Her mind had swirled all night, her heart rattling loudly in its cage. She allowed herself to skip her stretches and started the coffee instead. While it was gurgling she did her makeup. Shaky hands dogged her efforts.

She slipped into a plain gray nylon sweater, which she thought contrasted her dark makeup and made her look younger and more striking. For her bottoms, she chose a basic polyester pant that gave her the feeling she was really going somewhere.

Tapping her foot nervously, she sat at the table and drank endless cups of coffee to kill time. Four stories down, below the small patio beyond the kitchen counter, the construction workers were arriving; soon they'd resume erecting their building on the other side of the street, a structure she knew she'd loathe and which would block her view of the mountain. At eighty-eight years old, she felt she deserved more.

But she wouldn't let that bother her today. Nor would she dwell on the missing card she needed to play a proper game of solitaire. Nor on the runny eggs that were delivered for breakfast.

Nothing would ruin the excitement of the phone call to come at 8 a.m.

Finally, *finally* the clock with the cat eyes that glanced back and forth on each tick tock clicked to 7:55 a.m. Olivia opened the tablet case and spun the screen around to face her. It turned on, lit up, and scanned her face before opening to reveal her apps over the background picture of her and Little Jim, taken when he was just a few weeks old. They looked almost unreal in front of Matterhorn Mountain at Disneyland, as if their faces had been cut and pasted from another image.

The clock moved to 7:58 a.m.

Her finger shook over the button that read JOIN MEETING. The button was grayed-out, its color dimmed. Why these things had to be on a set schedule boggled her—as if the app company couldn't schedule this meeting at any old time. She was the client, wasn't she? In her day the companies had to cater to you, not the other way around.

When the clock turned to 8 a.m., she was ready. The grayed-out button turned blue, and she stabbed at it—but missed. She gasped, horrified she may have accidentally ruined the meeting. Thankfully, her terror was short-lived. The button remained where it was, and when her shaking subsided she tapped again, this time with a better aim.

The face, the glowing face of her wonderful Little Jim appeared. For the briefest of moments—almost too fast for the eye—his background flashed into white before returning.

Olivia felt herself melt at the sight of her sixteen-year-old grandson. He had perfectly white teeth and oval brown eyes. He was delighted to see her. His delight was contagious. She grinned. It was a miracle. The boy, the technology that made all this possible. Her heart swelled.

Grandma, how are you? Little Jim leaned close to the camera.

My boy, I'm wonderful. Just look at you. Look at how handsome you are.

Did you stretch this morning, Grandma?

He's so considerate, she thought. Always asking about

me. And how is school? she asked.

Jim smiled and held up a piece of paper. I just got my report card. And guess what?

She could hardly contain herself. She knew what was coming. But she asked anyway: What is it?

He flipped the paper around. Straight A's!

Her mouth dropped in fake surprise.

And an A plus in Statistics, he said. Thanks to you tutoring me.

Yes! Her eyes glinted. An A plus. I knew you could do it!

It's all because of you, Grandma!

A woman thirty years the boy's senior leaned into frame. Olivia could have wept on the spot. Her daughter; every day somehow more radiant than the last. Just returned from—

Cincinnati, Ma. The convention went amazingly well. I sold six hundred units; my publisher is so happy, they're offering me twice the advance of the last book. Oh, and one more thing . . .

Olivia held her breath in suspense as her daughter panned the camera down, revealing the tiniest bump—

Olivia's hand went to her mouth.

You're going to be a grandmother again. I'm four months along.

An upswell of joy nearly made the old lady faint. Here was her family—her fine family—all happy and healthy and smart and gorgeous, and they loved her. *They really loved her.* Growing up, she had dreamt that one day she'd leave a legacy like this. Too often over the years she'd seen friends whose families had gradually forgotten them as they drew closer to the earth. The fortunes they'd amassed through hard work, the combined efforts of them and their partners, dwindling, as the next generation swindled them for all they were worth.

But not her.

She smiled. Look at my family, she said to herself. Just look at them.

They talked for a half-hour about Olivia and her routine there at the nursing facility, and they made plans for the family to travel and see her, and when they were able to afford the larger house next year, why, they would just move her there to live out the rest of her days with them. Of course they would! All Olivia would have to do is come. They wouldn't take no for an answer.

I wouldn't want to be a burden, Olivia said.

That's ridiculous, her daughter said. How could you be a burden? We love you too much to be without you. You'll come here and we'll take care of you and you won't have to worry about anything. You can read all day and sit with the dachshund and watch the wild rabbits on the golf course through the window. We want to pay you back for all the years you raised us, all that time Dad was sick and you so selflessly took care of him. We would have suggested this before, but we weren't sure we could afford it—

Olivia wept. Oh, there's no need to apologize. Of course I'll come. Of course I will.

She was sure, this was it: the happiest moment of her life. No more enduring her grouchy, grumbling neighbor who complained about her late-night showers, how they could hear the pipes through the walls. No more prepackaged meals, hallways that stank of bleach, or gossipy busybodies in the library downstairs when she was trying to read. They—her family—would rescue her from all that, and the rest of her years would be the finest of all.

She closed her eyes, her chin quivering.

When she opened them, the application had flickered and frozen on the distorted faces of the ones she loved. Then their faces dropped off altogether. The screen turned black. Only the Family™ logo remained.

No! I thought I had another hour left.

A message flashed. She scrambled for her reading glasses. PLEASE UPDATE YOUR PAYMENT INFO TO CONTINUE.

Spitting, Olivia stabbed another button on the screen.

Finally, realizing what had happened, she pulled up the contact list stored on her tablet and scrolled until she found the right number.

It rang three times before Dani picked up on the video chat.

Her face was stone cold. "Mom."

"Did you cancel my Family™ account? Well, did you?"

Dani braced herself. "Our therapist said it was for the best—"

"Your *what?*"

"You heard me, Mom. Stop pretending." She drew a deep breath, ready to try again. "Our therapist said we need to stop paying for your games."

"Games!"

"It isn't healthy for you to be on those apps all the time, spending all day with that fake family. You already have a family. We're right here, Mom. We're only two hours away, for Christ's sake." She lowered her gaze, mouth trembling. "Why do you refuse to see us? You won't let us come over for birthdays or holidays. All you do is go on those apps that cost us hundreds of dollars a month—"

"It's none of your business what I do!"

"No. No, I guess not. But we also don't have to pay for it. Not when you have a perfectly good family that loves you. Delilah's eight now, you know that? She doesn't understand why her grandmother hasn't seen her in three years. She misses you. She needs you."

"You have no right," Olivia said. Her heart was racing, her nervous system on overdrive.

"Why won't you see us? Why do you spend all day replaying the same scenes over and over?"

"You'll be sorry," Olivia said softly.

"Mom—!"

Olivia tapped a red button. The meeting ended. Sitting in the stony silence of the room, she thought of Little Jim, who could always be counted on. She missed him and his mother terribly. Her eyes watered as the digital pictures of her Family™ faded from their frames around the house, forever deleted, leaving a short, fleeting impression on the black screen.

She contemplated how to fix her account; her payments were managed by those busybody good-for-nothings. She hardly knew how to work the app, in any case.

Outside the construction workers banged away. Olivia checked the clock, which read 8:56 a.m., then withdrew a pen and paper from her desk.

"You'll be sorry," she repeated to no one, and began plotting her revenge.

Man of Stone

GRIZZLED AND MANGLED, THE TROOPER BURST IN,
   Gore and waste running down his limbs.
Wrenching forward, his steps harried and tortured,
   He collapsed upon the floor of my inn.

"My partner," he cried, "was seized on the rocks—
   "The man of stone has snatched him as fare.
"Get horsed! Please ride! And rescue my friend—
   "In return you shall earn what money I bear!"

My stomach, it seized. For years I had heard
   Tales of the great stone beast under the moor.
Yet pistol in hand, I left that poor man

And trembled on my way out the door.

My gelding, Winston, drew in his breath,
    In shaky and shuddery fright.
Steeling our nerves, I kicked at his side
    And drove us deep into that viscous night.

I cannot tell of the bone-deep fear
    That feasted then upon my soul.
The wind off the fen—again and again
    Took my mind and my wits for its toll.

Yet still we pressed on, and miles we fled,
    Milky dense fog swarming my brain.
Abruptly we stopped, and Winston reared up
    The moor's edge mere feet from his mane.

Beneath us then moved the rubbled ground—
    A great rock flexed a gargantuan hand.
'Twas then that I knew, the stories were true—
    The stone man was alive under our land!

Its craggy visage, more ancient and wasted
    Than the blackest depths of unknown space.
It wore a hungry grin, with teeth made of tin,
    That had chewed up men of every race.

The sea roiled up, the sky split asunder,
    A loathsome cackle boomed askew.
In the palm of a hand, the rock gripping a man,
    Who shrieked as he was pulled down and through.

The moor fell dark, the rocks settled and stilled.

Not a click or a clack could I hear.
I called as I lurched, so long did I search,
   Yet no trace of the man did appear.

So today I stand watch, for any who come
   Who would tread upon my family's black land.
Ye who do dare, ye are warned—so beware!
   Of the one we call the giant stone man.

Jack Nasty on the Wind

THE RINGING PHONE PULLED ME FROM A DEEP slumber. It was the kind of dreamy darkness from which it takes will and energy to emerge, like swimming up from the bottom of a murky lagoon.

Groggily, I put the receiver to my ear.

"Charles?" A thin, raspy voice. Barely above a whisper. A woman's voice. "It's Mercedes. From down the road."

Her last sentence sounded like a question. *Do you remember me?*

I sat up. The breeze drifted in, carrying with it the smell of fresh hay. The clock read 2:38 a.m. I waited for her to continue, but she just breathed.

I crossed the room to the window facing west. Peeled back the window shade and gazed across the corn field at her large, two-story brick house. The lights were off.

Strange, her calling me. Mercedes had come into the hardware store a few times, and we'd had a pleasant conversation or two since she moved here five months ago. But that was all.

I politely asked her what she was doing, calling me so darn late.

Several times she started to speak, then stopped. I heard her swallow dryly.

"He's found me," she whispered. "I don't know how, but he has. Someone's gotta know. Someone's gotta know I wasn't crazy."

I squinted out the window. I was far away, sure, but still I didn't see anything wrong at the house. I asked who she was talking about.

She took a long time to answer.

"He's back. Jack Nasty is back."

The phone crackled. I tapped on the receiver, but the line was already dead.

I threw on my jacket and tromped down the driveway onto the road leading to Mercedes's house. I brought my heaviest flashlight but didn't think to grab my gun. In hindsight, I should have, even if what ended up happening never did. It could have been a jealous ex-boyfriend that had come calling; in which case, being armed would've been smart. But it didn't come to that, and as it turned out, it might not have done much good anyway.

It's been windy all week, and earlier tonight it was downright howling. Its screaming across the plains here is something else, not like other places. No, Nebraska's different. Cornfields rippling back and forth like the top of an ocean. I don't know if it was my imagination, or if I was feeling strange because of the phone call, but on that walk over I had the sudden urge to turn and run far, far away. It made no sense, but that's how it was. Nothing but dread in my belly. I felt like I was walking straight into a black hole. Twice I almost clicked on my flashlight, but some little voice inside me told me not to. Like it was going to draw the attention of something if I did. So I pushed those thoughts aside and kept going.

The road hooked around. The house came into view. It was still dark inside.

I went up to the porch. I knocked and called for Mercedes. I heard nothing. I knocked again.

A flurry of wind blasted the house. The hairs on my neck stood as something cold blew down my back. My teeth began to chatter, and I spun around like I expected to find someone tickling me.

Nobody was there, of course.

As I looked out, the clouds parted overhead and a knife's arc of moonlight flashed across the cornfield, illuminating three dim figures standing roughly equal distance from each other.

I squinted. They were scarecrows. Common things. I thought nothing of it. I turned to knock again but Mercedes had opened the door. Her face was already poking through the small gap there, her stringy hair blowing about her like wispy cotton strands.

"Do you see them?" she croaked. Her eyes glinted in the light.

I looked around. "There's no one here, Mercedes."

She pointed a crooked finger through the door.

"*Them*," she said.

I followed her point.

"The scarecrows?" I said. "They're yours. Came with the property, yeah?"

"Only two of 'em did. Third one ain't mine. The middle one there."

I stared. Tried to get a read on her. From the tequila I smelled on her breath, I was pretty sure what I was dealing with.

"Will you take me?" Her voice got louder. "Just drive me away from here?" She gestured into the house behind her. Several bulky bags were lying on the floor. "I'm all packed."

I told her I would be happy to drive her in the morning, anywhere she wanted to go, the bus station or even the airport, but in the meantime she needed to sleep it off. You know how booze can take hold of people, especially in rural, more remote places like Bartlett here. And I was in no mood to co-sign a drinker's delusions tonight. Plus I was getting irritable; I was gonna have to open the store in a few hours.

She began to cry, begging me to take her right then. "Please," she said, "I don't have a car, and I won't make it till morning alive. I just know it." She looked like someone yanked from the sea after a shipwreck—drifting, frozen, terrified of everything *out there*. She must have been no more than eighty pounds; her flimsy night dress barely grasping her skinny puppy frame.

But I wasn't gonna budge. Wasn't gonna take her all the way to the train station tonight, it being two hours each way. Not when I had to open the store so early, and I needed my sleep.

Her eyes went big then, and she reached out and

grabbed my arm and wrenched me inside. She'd seen something behind me, I realize now. Quick as lightning she slammed the door behind me and locked the deadbolt. Her grip was viselike and her fingers icy. She spun me around.

"Look!"

I was face to face with the little square window in the door. My eyes settled. I scanned the cornfields. The rising wind pummeled the house. Dust swirled everywhere.

Out there, in the bending corn stalks, I could see the three scarecrows.

"He's moving," Mercedes whispered, her face next to mine. I recoiled at the rank stench. She was dehydrated, and stank badly. "The middle one. That's Jack."

I stared at the figure in the center. Maybe it was my imagination—hard to say—but it looked . . . closer than before. Maybe. Could have been a trick of the moonlight, I thought. Some weird reflection skipping off the corn rows like a flat stone on water.

Another burst of wind rocked the house. The wooden frame creaked loudly. An old place, I remembered; the foundation was set way back in the late 1800s. As long as I've lived here, no real work has been done on it.

Mercedes shrank to the floor then, her hands clutching her head. The sounds of the wind seemed to terrify her. The veins in her arms were like heavy rivers. Lines of blood formed where her fingernails dug in and raked down her face. She cried. Her sobs pulled her into a fetal position. I wanted to comfort her, but something inside told me to let her be for a moment, that there was something that needed to be exorcised, that it would be wrong to stop her.

I stepped away to give her some space and fill up a glass of water from the kitchen sink. The dishes were in piles. They had not been done in a long time. Food and broken plates crunched underfoot. I heard the scuttling of roaches.

I returned to the living room and handed her the glass. She gulped it down in a couple big swallows. "It's too late," she said. "If the wind keeps up, I'll be gone by morning." Her eyes went wide. "You should go, else he comes for you next."

I nodded like I was considering it. I wasn't. Ashamed to say now that I didn't believe her. It was clear to me she needed someone to stay with her till she sobered up or went to bed. Poor lady was liable to kill herself. I wasn't exactly sure what to do, but I decided that keeping her talking was smart.

I pointed to the pictures on the wall, the ones of Mercedes as a young woman holding up skulls in front of what looked to be excavation sites.

"Montana." She stared blankly. "Ten, twelve years ago. Back when I was a bone hunter."

"An anthropologist," I said.

"That's right."

"Where'd you study?"

"University of Pennsylvania."

"Why anthropology?"

"I don't know . . . I guess because I like stories. The bones, they tell stories. Stories of time, energy. That's all it really is, in the end. Anthropology, I mean. Time and energy."

She drew a deep breath. Her shoulders relaxed. Talking seemed to be helping. I asked her to continue, to tell me more about her time there. She pulled up a bottle of Jose Gold from behind the couch and swigged it.

"There was a dig in Montana," she said. "In the badlands. Where everything's hot and jagged. We were on a private search for a rich guy out there, for a museum probably, so he could get his name up on the display and have a wing named after him.

"One day we came across a large slit in the desert. Like a cut in the earth. Later we were told it had been a sacred spot for the Indians who once lived there. We went into the slit, maybe fifty feet down. We didn't find much, mostly bits of shredded clothes and some scattered bones, but we did find one thing of interest. A green gemstone. A sunstone, it's called. It was beautiful. It had an endless quality to it, like you could gaze into it forever and never get to the bottom of it.

"A few days later, an old native I met told me a legend about that place. I thought he was just trying to scare me. But when I showed him the stone, he begged me to get rid of it, to throw it back into the slit . . . or to the bottom of the ocean.

"The way he told it, when white men first came to this country, there was a pilgrim, see, a man named Jack Nasty, who tore across the land, killing, murdering, burning villages to the ground. He wore a pilgrim's hat, but he wasn't a Puritan. No, that was a ruse. In fact, he was a practitioner of the old ways, of the dark wisdom, who commanded squirmy things and the putrid and nameless terrors that once haunted primordial man. One night during a raid on a Cheyenne tribe, an arrow struck him down. As he died, he imprisoned his own soul in a green sunstone.

"Of course, I thought it was just a story, no different from the ones I heard every day in my field. You hear a lot of strange things, you know. Everyone has some tale. So I didn't think much of it.

"But a few days later, something strange happened. The necklace became very heavy around my neck. My mind grew foggy. Suddenly, I had an overwhelming urge to smash the gem on the rocks. It seemed to me an odd thing to do, but the urge was overpowering. Something had to be done. My mind raced. I didn't know why. I curse myself now, for it wasn't me thinking these thoughts! It was the gem; or, rather, what was inside the gem, that was telling me to do it.

"I went back to the farm where I was staying. I set the gem on the large boulder near the scarecrow there and smashed it with a rock. It cracked, and some of it split off and flew into dust.

"I felt better. I went inside and fell into a deep sleep. I woke up early the next morning for work, feeling good and rested. The other bone hunters I was staying with were still asleep. I got in my car and made the drive to my dig an hour north.

"I didn't think much of it then, but I noticed when I left that the scarecrow that was mounted on the edge of the field where I'd smashed the stone was missing. Like it walked right off its stake. I figured maybe the McKendrick boys down the road had stolen it—they were always playing pranks like that—or maybe one of the farmhands was patching it up. Either way, it had been there the day before, and was gone the next morning.

"I drove to work, feeling good about getting an early start. I did my job. When I returned home, though, I found the place swarming with police."

She slumped. "All four of my housemates had been killed. Their bodies, strewn all over. Police said each of them had been running from their attacker as he hacked them apart."

She swallowed hard, blinking back tears. "But the worst part, the part no one could explain, was the bits of straw in all the blood and . . . the entrails. It was everywhere, even in my bedroom." She exhaled shakily. "I knew it, then. I know how crazy it sounds, but I *knew* then that Jack Nasty had come looking for me. I *knew* he was in that scarecrow. That I had released him from the gem. And he wanted me. That's how it works. That's why the native had told me to get rid of it, quick. Once you release him, he comes for you and kills anyone in his way. He had come looking for me—and would come again.

"I was pretty shook up after that. One of the officers let me stay with his family for a few days. I lived there and recovered, shaken but grateful I was alive.

"Yet again I had a strange instinct, a few days later, when the policeman left for his night shift. I believe strongly in intuition, and also in warnings from other realms, and all at once I had another urge, this time to leave, to hop a train and get as far away as possible.

"I glanced out the window then, as the moon flashed over the yard. A pale figure stood there. It swayed in the breeze, and during the next gust of wind, I swore it moved closer to the house.

"It was the scarecrow, the one from the house where my friends had been murdered. It had been carried by the wind. It must have been. How else is a scarecrow supposed to move around? Well, that was quite enough for me. I grabbed the officer's wife's keychain and stole the car. Glancing in the rearview mirror as I was leaving, I saw the crooked smile painted on the face not ten feet from me! It was still following me—on the wind!

"I drove until the tank was dry, then hitched a ride to the next train station. From there I just kept going. For five years I moved around, staying one step ahead, before settling here. Stupid me, I thought it was over. I thought maybe, just maybe, I'd imagined the whole thing. It had been so long, after all. There was no way the wind could carry him back to me . . ." She sank into herself.

"But that's it. I can't run anymore. I'm too old, too tired. And tonight, when I looked out the window and saw it, I called you, I suppose, so that I could tell someone what was happening. So someone would know the truth."

Silence fell over the house. I reached out and set a hand on her shoulder, to let her know I was there. Even if I didn't believe her story, I believed that she believed.

If I knew then what I know now, would I have done anything differently? I like to think I would have, but— what? What was there to do?

Hell, I don't know.

I just don't know.

An enormous gale rocked the house then, breaking my thoughts. The lamp flickered and went out. Power failure. The house was bathed in darkness.

Mercedes turned. Her face pressed against the window in the door.

She gasped.

"What is it?" I stood beside her and peered out. The two scarecrows were staked on either side of the field, but the third—the one in the middle—*was gone.*

"The wind blew it over," I said. "That's all. I'll go out. I'll show you."

"No!" She let out a ghastly yell as I set my hand on

the doorknob.

Above us, we heard a crash. A shattering of glass on another floor. She whipped her head up.

"The attic window," she whispered.

"A tree branch must have fallen and broke it," I said.

Neither of us spoke. She began to whimper. An unconscious move on her part. She was overtaken by shivers. Trembling, she nearly collapsed on the couch, but stabilized herself with a locked wrist.

The floor above us creaked. The house groaned.

Something was walking up there.

Mercedes's voice went thin and reedy. "The wind has blown it onto the roof. And he's crawled inside the house!"

I gripped the flashlight at my side. I did not breathe; I did not move. A cold sweat broke out over my arms.

God almighty, I thought, whatever walks up there doesn't breathe.

But no. Another voice took hold. This was not real. There was nothing up there, nothing at all. Vengeful straw men do not exist, do not blow in the wind, and do not stalk women across the plains!

"Christ." She shuddered horribly and gripped my arm until her fingers were white. She could not tear her eyes from the ceiling. We shrank from the shuffling above us. It sounded as if two near-weightless feet were dragging themselves across the cedar-wood floors. The sound was airy and light, but definite.

I clicked on my flashlight and went timidly toward the staircase that led to the next floor. The blood seemed to have drained from my body. Mercedes tiptoed next to me, her breath ragged. My mind screamed at me to run.

But if we left then, Mercedes would have gone back to

wandering the lands alone, dodging some maniacal manifestation of her mind, or worse. And I would never know the truth. But I had to know. We all do. Everyone must test, at certain times, their own beliefs in the things that linger in the crevices of the earth and survive beyond the moonlight.

You know for sure demons don't exist? That other realms were invented by men and women in order to make sense of the real world?

I did.

Yes. Once, I did, too.

The floor moaned as we set foot on the stairs. I gripped the banister. I was sure the thing in the attic could hear every step. We were naked, exposed, and yet— and yet—there was no such thing as a walking scarecrow.

I remember nothing of the walk up those stairs. I recall setting foot at the top of the landing and turning to my right, down the darkened hall. There was a little moonlight streaming in but nothing more. I was shaking hard. Something primordial inside me had been set off like an alarm.

Halfway down the hall on the second floor, we stopped under the pull-down attic door, the kind that folds into a ladder. The house murmured as I grasped the cord. I gathered all my reserves of energy, of willpower, of sanity, and pulled to release the door.

A faceless brown thing lurched from the darkness.

It grabbed the screaming Mercedes. With an inhuman grip, it reared back, wrenching her from her spot and hauling her into the abyss above. I fell backward, stupidly scrabbling for something—anything —to hold. By the time I leapt up from the floor, I could do nothing to try and beat back the ghoul and save the poor lady, for the attic door had sprung into its locked position, sealing them inside.

A muffled voice howled in the darkness. It was quickly choked off. Then, silence. The lack of sound rooted me still for a moment. I didn't breathe. Finally, I forced myself to snatch the cord and pull it down. Ghoul be damned! I extended the ladder rungs and raced up.

A broken body lay on the floor. Mercedes's brown hair swirled messily around her head. Her neck was unnaturally bent and her eyes bulging. Her tongue unfurled uselessly against the side of her mouth, her hands claw-like on the floor. Her nails had broken down to the quick, and blood reddened her fingertips.

Cold air blasted at me from the window.

My mind froze and I saw images, still ones only, of her rigid body, her frozen scream, the trail of straw, the open window, and the faint outline of a wispy figure in the blustery sky, drifting like an errant bird searching for its next worm.

Lonely One

If you really want to know, I left the hospital because I found the amount of despair there totally lacking. The guards were too friendly, the doctors too hellbent on caring and helping and all that jizzum. I just wanted to be left alone. Apparently, that was too much to ask. Worst of all, they spoiled us with too much food and too many pills. It was so good, it plain stopped working for me. So when I finally escaped in the back of that laundry truck, I set out with one goal in mind: to experience my internal limits in the fearsome land of loneliness.

I could have gone to some isolated place, somewhere

in the mountains or the desert. But a million dopey adventurers had already done that, proven by their idiotic pictures that magazines seemed to love. They'd already conquered it all. There was nothing left for me.

Anyway, what I wanted would have no picture at the end, no final proof of victory. My last moment would be purely Pyrrhic, which I hoped would only increase the misery and desolation.

No, to be truly alone, you have to be in a busy place. Paradoxically, the more people one surrounds himself with, the lonelier he can become. Cities, with their nasty smells and sloppy heat, make a melancholic experience much deeper and more sensuous. When people are near, but you're still alone, well, isn't that the saddest state of all?

It called me. I had to have it. I set out for oblivion.

What better place than Los Angeles?

THE STUDIO APARTMENT WAS PERFECT, WAY BETTER THAN what I imagined at the hospital. Four hundred feet square, it had a fridge and a little electric burner which I promptly dismantled. I snuck that downstairs to the dumpster and then sold the fridge for a little cash.

The place was infested with roaches that scattered when I flipped on my little work lamp. Cracks in the walls ran like webs drawn by drunken spiders. The landlord took my deposit of two weeks up front. Didn't even ask for a credit or background check. And after finding some cheap clothes in the dumpster at one of the many thrift stores, I was ready to start my mission.

I LIKED HER DEMEANOR RIGHT AWAY. SHE'D SHOT THE photo of herself at a forty-five degree angle, from above, which seemed to be a typical format nowadays. Her smile was a little plastered on, which meant she felt uncomfortable. That was a good sign.

Her dating profile said she was new in town and looking to meet other new people. Her name was Aubrey, and she had curly brown hair. A streak of acne banding across her chin like a strap suggested a hormonal imbalance. Her home was probably filled with cheap furniture from a plug-n-play store, made from plastic slathered over glued wood chips. Maybe she had those pictures on her walls like I'd seen in Curtis's photos of his lady's house he used to hold up to my cell window, the ones with blitheringly stupid slogans on them like "In this house, we laugh and cry and fart and love each other" or whatever.

She looked like the perfect subject.

Besides, she was the only one who accepted my request for a date.

My dating profile, by the way, said that I worked as an IT security associate. Moron that he was, Curtis the orderly had armed me with some useful dating advice. He was constantly swiping on his phone and showing me which females he found most attractive, and why, and also told me that women today love "techies" because they tend to have money and smarts and all that.

"You have to look confident," he said. "Women like stability. Good prospects should have money. Oh, and they want children. All of them." He nodded solemnly when he said that, so I know he believed it. Even though he had a girlfriend, he used to spend six or seven hours of his shift swiping and looking, grading and rating and messaging and all that. When he went home in the morning he would be cross-eyed from the blue light.

Anyway—quick aside—one day he was babbling about how he would never get a real partner because of his horrible job, and was whining about his weight. He had all kinds of strange theories on the subject of women, and I was tired of listening to them. So one night I slipped some laxatives I'd tongued earlier into his soda. The pills cramped him up severely, and it was only weeks later when he stopped showing up for work that Doctor Klein told me that Curtis had succumbed to kidney failure and expired.

I think I may have been confused and gave him a mega dose of lithium by accident.

But who knows.

I LOGGED OFF MY ACCOUNT AT THE LIBRARY COMPUTER, which I reserved after lifting a card from the purse of an old lady I helped cross the street near the supermarket. If the authorities ever track my search history, they'll find Heather Jennings with a lot to answer for, I'll tell you that. I only hope that the raid will inspire in her a great terror, for the old people of America live in a vast solitude I can only dream of.

I ARRIVED AT THE COFFEE SHOP AT 6:15 P.M. OUR DATE WAS at 6:00, but it's best to let people wait. It's a little-known secret that people are more engaged when they have to work a little, especially when they have to work a little for another person. It's important they know they're not too important.

I sauntered over and tried to appear smoldering. Curtis said men should try to look smoldering.

Aubrey stood and smiled, and it was not an unpleasant set of teeth that poked out of her mouth. She was heavier than her picture suggested, which I liked, and her hand was sweaty, and she seemed nervous.

I slid into my seat and halfway smiled at her and pretended to be shy by looking away. Playing bashful, by the way, is important for establishing camaraderie quickly, since it portrays you as vulnerable. In doing so, you psychotronically ask your partner for help.

Like a good Samaritan, she tried to make me comfortable by asking if I wanted a coffee. That meant trust was already building between us. I began to relax.

I scoped her out while we talked. Her hair was mussed and greasy. Her face was chubby and sallow, like a droopy gray glove. Gapped teeth too, I noticed, which always adds character.

I liked her right away.

"I run the IT department at my company," I told her. "It's a . . . well, I shouldn't say too much. It's a government thing, you know."

"Oh."

"I don't want to get you in trouble. You understand."

"No. Of course not."

"And you?"

"I'm a vet tech."

"Heh?"

"A vet tech. I take care of sick animals, do house calls, things like that. Sometimes I have to go to people's homes and put their animals down, when they're terminal."

"Do you have to express their glands?"

"Sometimes." She perked up. "It's one of my main jobs."

Well, this was interesting. Dying animals. Squeezing their glands. Maybe she was hiding more misery than I thought.

"How do you do it?" I asked.

"You're interested in this? Like, actually interested?"

I picked up my glass, stared at it, then set it down. "Yes. Yes, I am."

"You should really have two people," she explained, mimicking with her hands. "One in the back, one in the front, that way the dog doesn't get finicky and try to run. It isn't very comfortable for them."

"I can imagine."

"Then you have to put on a glove and reach inside with two fingers. You may have to move the fecal matter aside to find the gland. Then you squeeze until it all drains out."

"And you mop it up?"

"You try to catch it all with a towel."

"Tell me." I leaned in. "Is it a lonely job?"

She thought. "Sometimes. I guess it can be very lonely."

"You put animals down a lot?"

"Yeah."

"And you don't know many people here in Los Angeles."

"Not many." She looked down at her murky coffee. "A few coworkers. They're not really friends, though."

"Are you sad?"

"Sad? I guess so."

"But that's how you like it."

She shrugged. "Doesn't everybody?"

Surprised, I sat back.

Doesn't everybody? Doesn't everybody like to be sad? Well, no, obviously not. Not at the hospital, anyway. That's why they kept me there: I was "too sad." Of course, I wanted to be sad. They just wouldn't let me.

But Aubrey . . . Was she like me? Did we have something in common, a shared bond? Did she really like to be lonely as much as I did?

I let the silence hang for a minute or so, pretending to admire the pictures on the wall of the shapeless figures in black and white that moved blobbily in their video frames. They were the epitome of wretchedness— little blank-faced men caught in some socialist regime. That would have been a good life for me: everything laid out and organized so I didn't have to think at all. I was born in the wrong time and place, that's for sure.

I wasn't sure what to say, so I just sat there. Aubrey, too. She seemed to be thinking hard. White crust had gathered at the corners of her mouth as she talked to herself, her face all scrunched in the palm of her hand, her elbow jammed into the table.

Finally, she looked up. With a resigned sigh, she said, "Well, do you want to see my father's grave?"

IF YOU HAVEN'T RIDDEN THE BUS LATELY IN A BIG CITY, you owe it to yourself to take one and cruise. It had been decades for me, but it had lost none of the ickiness, stickiness, and despondency I remembered. It felt like the old days again: Mom slamming my butt down in the seat, wagging her ugly bent finger in my face and saying, "Now you sit here until five o'clock and not a minute before. If you leave, I'll know. These people all work for me, and they'll call me if you do. Now take your sandwich and banana. No, don't kiss me goodbye. You know the rules. And don't talk to anybody. If you do, they'll call me . . ."

Those wonderful sensations of dread and terror came

flooding back. Aubrey seemed to sense I wanted to sit in my feelings, because she was quiet the whole way to the cemetery, too. Maybe she felt the same way I did.

When we arrived, I followed her off the bus and through the open gate, into the sea of gravestones. She led me through an open hole in the fence at the back of the lot. We had to push through a tangle of trees and branches, and by the time we reached the small unmarked stone in a small clearing, streaks of red were running down my face.

"We paid a lot for this spot," she said. "It's the only place that was secluded enough for Dad."

"There's no name on the stone."

"We decided it would be lonelier if we omitted it." She looked down and said softly: "It's what he would have wanted."

I thought it would be rude to tell her that by fulfilling his wish, she had paradoxically only increased his posthumous sense of comfort and wellbeing. But I let it go and said nothing.

She stood over the grave, staring blankly, so I circled the perimeter of trees, putting heel to toe slowly and methodically all the way around. We didn't speak. I wondered what she was thinking. Hopefully she was relishing her misery. I gave her space, respectfully, to enjoy it.

On my tenth or eleventh loop around, I glanced up to find her walking away. She hadn't said goodbye. I waited another few laps before stumbling back through the brambles and into the cemetery. When I emerged, she was gone.

As I left the cemetery I realized I was lost. I hadn't paid attention to the route the bus had taken. Also, I hadn't brought any money, except for a small handful of pennies and nickels in my pocket.

I walked the streets. A vagrant sprang out of an alley to rob me, but I had no money and he had no sense, so we parted ways amicably.

I didn't ask for directions. I wanted to. But of course I would not. The negation of desire was the point of all this, and I'd come to live. Eventually the sun woke me up on the street somewhere, and wouldn't you know it: I had unconsciously wandered and collapsed just three blocks from my apartment. The memory is a marvelous thing, I thought, as I grabbed a handful of old newspapers off the stoop to use as toilet paper upstairs.

I CHECKED THE DATING SITE TWO DAYS LATER, BUT I couldn't find Aubrey's profile. It seemed to have vanished. Had she erased it? I felt numb, shocked, at first. That gave way to sadness, and I indulged it. I cried. I couldn't remember any woman making me feel that much. I felt like I'd been left, dumped, ditched—and it was everything I'd come here for. All I could think about was finding her again, but she was gone and that was the point.

Weeks passed and my feelings stayed. Rain from a passing storm flooded my apartment, intensifying the loneliness. The strongest Los Angeles rain in half a century. Gray water pooled around my toilet, in my tub, down the faded brick walls in the living area. I watched it all while relishing the sorrow.

Day after day, I continued checking my dating profiles. Still no word from Aubrey. When I grew tired of that I sat at bus stops. I faced west in the mornings, keeping the sun at my back for effect, and east in the afternoon. Sometimes I wrapped myself in newspaper and begged for change. To my pleasure I found that no one carried change anymore. So much had been modernized since I'd been hospitalized.

As for the hospital, I'd stopped worrying about them finding me. I hadn't used my name since I climbed out of the laundry truck and wasn't sure how else they could track me down. To be honest, I was a bit disappointed they hadn't. But I decided, after some thought, that it was better this way. I had come here for the Supreme Loneliness, after all, right?

Following that thought came another. A scary one.

What if I wasn't caught?

What if I had . . . a future?

I had never thought about that. I figured I'd be on my own for a week or two before the hospital goons crashed in my door and dragged me back. But it had already been a month. And they hadn't come.

So, I was here now. I could either keep going, dive deeper into the experience—or turn myself in.

But wait. Now there was a third option. I could give up this loneliness bit and get a job. Or a home.

I froze.

A job?

A home?

A . . . wife?

Those dreaded words. The signifiers of stability. The things I swore I would never pursue.

But there they were.

Good God, what was wrong with me? Did I have a fever? Had I lost my mind?

I CHECKED THE DATING SITES UP TO TWENTY TIMES A DAY.

I had to ask her what she thought. Could we be happy together? Was it possible? Could two miserable wretches like us actually build something together? Or was it all a fantasy? Maybe she had moved on with her life already and forgotten all about me.

I did my best to track her down. I called every veterinary hospital in the greater Los Angeles area, but could find no tech named Aubrey. No one even matched her description, so far as they would tell me.

I stalked the streets and peered into the windows of every coffee shop I found. I screamed incoherently at anyone who would listen to me.

Finally, in desperation, I found myself at the cemetery, pushing my way back through the bramble branches and feeling the familiar streaks on my face. I plopped down in the center of the clearing. I would wait until she returned to visit her father. Even if I died, at least she would eventually find my body stretched out over the grave, fingers and nails digging into the earth.

And who could ever forget that?

ON THE THIRD DAY I RAN OUT OF WATER.

Determined to die, I began to dig up her father's casket. The recent storm had abruptly given way to a horrible heat wave. The earth was dry and crumbling. Refusing to find a stick with which to dig, I used my hands. By the end of that day I had gone about four feet. The heat almost did me in. I woke up the next morning, weak, with a blistering headache, but encouraged enough by my progress to continue.

By mid-afternoon I had dug another two or three feet, but still had not found the coffin. I wouldn't let that stop me. I kept going.

I must have passed out again, because the next thing I knew the sun was beginning its climb, the light skimming the top of the grave. I was nine feet deep or so by then; I reached my hands up but could no longer grasp the top edge of the grave.

I crumpled to the ground, too weak to move.

I CAN'T TELL HOW LONG I'VE BEEN HERE. THE SUN NO longer reaches me. I am close to the Ultimate Despair.

Aubrey has not returned, for this is not her father's real grave. I know that now. Maybe she has no father at all. I've been played, strung along, discarded by someone better at the Game than I was.

BUT THEN I LOOK UP. A FIGURE FORMS. IT'S FUZZY. LOOKS like Aubrey. Could be. Her hands, set on her hips. Gazing at me in pity. Or is it guilt?

I smile at the thought.

She's so close now. Not close enough though. She can't reach down to pull me to safety. She disappears. Reappears. Scrambling for a ladder? Too late.

Loneliness has overtaken me. I feel it exploding from my chest. A bursting nebula. I taste my tears. Pain. Exquisite pain.

She probably came after seeing my last profile update: AUBREY, THIS IS FOR U. I CAN'T LIVE WITHOUT YOU. PLEASE FIND ME, YOU KNOW WHERE.

I feel relieved. Life ending. In front of the person closest to me. While she looks down, lovingly, caringly. On hands and knees now. Screaming for me. My vision —going dark.

There is. No better Feeling. Than this.

My love. Is there. Right there. I cannot touch her. She is too far.

She will not reach me.

But she cares.

She really cares.

I have won.

In The Trees
(*A Fairy Tale*)

THEY SAT ON THE BED, PEERING OUT THE WINDOW at the fan palm tree whose top danced seemingly miles above the head of the young boy.

"What's up there?" the boy asked. "At the top of the trees?"

"Monkeys."

He looked at his father sideways. "Yeah, right."

"I'm telling you the truth, Caleb. They steal people and take them up there."

"They do? They take kids?" His eyes were wide.

"No, silly. Only adults. When they die, they're taken into the trees."

"Nah ah. They didn't take Mom."

"You don't believe me, then?"

Caleb crossed his arms.

"Oh, it's real," Harry Carr said. "See, when kids grow up, they get old in spirit—wait, you know what that means, don't you?"

Caleb shrugged.

"It means they forget how to have fun. Their minds become full with jobs and bills and taxes; they become so distracted that they can no longer use their imagination. It's the worst thing that can happen to an adult."

"It is?"

"Oh, yes. They get old and crusty and calcified and frown a lot, and they forget all about the monkeys in the trees. They're too bitter to remember that life used to be about having fun, and about living, and about believing in ridiculous things."

They watched the branches sway a while longer. Caleb thought the tree might fall over from all the wind, and he meant to stay awake to see it happen, but soon he was asleep and his father had left the room.

CALEB GREW UP AND DID WHAT MOST PEOPLE DO, WHICH IS grow old in spirit and forget how to have fun. He became old and crusty and calcified. His life revolved around bills for this and payments for that, and oil changes for the car, and then there were his taxes, and his mortgage, and his career, and he forgot all about the monkeys in the trees and what happens when people die.

He learned of his father's death the day after a big promotion at work. They hadn't spoken in many years; some dispute over politics, he recalled. He got the call from the notifier at the hospital, and he emailed his boss, and he showered and dressed, and he vacantly stared as he drove the four hundred miles back home.

There was nobody to greet him as he entered. The house was dark and quiet.

The picture of Caleb that had sat on the little hallway table in the entryway since he was five was still there, jacketed in dust. The whole downstairs smelled musty, like a downtown thrift store. Hardcover books on everything from the tombs of Tutankhamen to the history of ore mining in South America lined the walls on brown wooden shelves. He opened the closet in the hallway and found it full of souvenirs and knick-knacks his father had collected on the cruises he'd taken during retirement.

He wandered around a while, absentmindedly peeking into the other rooms. There wasn't much to look at, or much to organize, or much to do, really. There was a television with cable in the living room, but there were no baseball games on and he didn't feel like channel surfing.

Caleb climbed the stairs to his old bedroom on the second floor. His father had replaced the twin bed many years earlier with a queen. Posters had long since been taken down, and the room repainted. New molding ran along the tops and bottoms of the walls. Everything had been fixed up, but it was still there in his memories, and as he sat on the bed and glanced outside he could again see the old palm tree swaying in the breeze.

He sat there, staring at it for some time, until the ringing of his phone brought him back. He answered. It was Paul, the owner of Reed Mortuary.

"I confirmed the funeral service tomorrow at three,

didn't I?" Caleb asked.

"Yes, but that's not why I called." Paul cleared his throat. "There's a problem."

Caleb waited.

"I don't know how to say this, but . . . well, this has never happened before." There was a pregnant pause. "Your father's body has . . . disappeared. Can you come down here? Right away?"

"I had just left your father in the embalming room," Paul explained to Caleb and the police officers. "I was about to dress him for tomorrow's service when the phone rang, so I left to answer it. I was finishing my call when I heard a scream. I rushed back in to see what had happened. But your father's body was just—gone. . . ."

The poor fellow was beside himself. He gripped his head with one hand and had to sit.

The police were stumped. None of them had heard of such a thing, not in their combined forty-seven years on the force.

There were only a few possibilities. First, Paul Reed or an accomplice had taken the body, and Paul was now making up a farfetched story as cover. But Caleb thought this unlikely. What possible motive could he have for stealing his father's body? Anyway, if Mr. Reed had done it, he was putting on quite an act of pretending to be distraught, tearing his hair out as he pleaded with the officer to find whoever did this.

The second option was Harry Carr got up and walked out. But bodies don't normally get up and stroll out of embalming stations.

The third option was someone or something else had taken it.

"You said you heard a scream?" Caleb asked.

"Yes," Paul said. "But it wasn't a human scream. It was an animal."

"You're sure?"

"Yes, sir. It was unmistakable."

"What kind of animal?"

Paul looked up, his eyes red and glassy. "A monkey," he said. "It sounded just like a howling monkey."

THE BED FRAME SQUEAKED AS CALEB SAT UP TO WATCH the palm tree.

The clock read 3:15 a.m. He had long since given up trying to sleep. Instead, he lazily watched the treetop sway. He had entered those strange hours of the night, where nothingness and reality and fantasy all collide and nothing makes sense but you don't care much because it's all so nice and dreamy and—

He looked again and squinted. Something was flickering . . .

Up there. In the trees.

Was that a light? A little yellow light? Like a flashlight?

It couldn't be. It must be a reflection or a plane or far-off office building or—

No. It was coming from inside the tree. It was shimmering and flickering, but not like someone waving a flashlight.

It looked like firelight.

Impossible, he thought.

Yet he was watching it with his own eyes, wasn't he?

He opened the window using the little crank and leaned out.

And heard it.

The howling of a monkey.

He stood at the base of the tree and stared up the tall trunk. The wind was roaring. It was impossible to tell if the faint *ooh ooh aah aahs* he heard were emanating from up above or from inside his mind.

He examined the tree. Notches and grooves in the bark led all the way up. It was as if perfect footholds had been placed there just for him. In fact, he could visualize the whole climb. In his mind's eye, he saw himself . . . going . . . up there. Hadn't he seen someone climb a palm tree before in some old film? Surely this would work the same way, right?

Just to test, just to see for himself how it would feel, he set his right hand against the trunk. Then he wrapped his left hand around and felt the grooves there. He bent his fingers and locked them into place.

He set the toes of his right foot against the trunk and stepped up onto a groove.

After a look at the glowing treetop, he set off up the trunk, one hand over the other. He found the climb to be remarkably easy.

When he was about twelve feet up, he paused and looked around. He felt no loss of strength. Might as well go up a little bit more, he thought.

Just to see.

Before he knew it, he was halfway up. The tree swayed fiercely. He swayed with it. He felt a bit like one of those captains on a ship in a storm. He could almost hear the yells of the pirates, feel the slap of the sea on his face.

Ooh ooh aah aah—

And the howling drifted down from the tree top.

Drawing his focus back, he started to climb again. It

took almost no effort. He marveled at the power he felt. His muscles were tight and lean. Normally, five minutes at the gym left him gasping for air, arms and legs screaming. But not tonight.

CALEB PULLED HIMSELF INTO THE NEST AT THE TOP OF the tree and pitched forward onto his belly. It was much bigger up here than he would have thought. There was plenty of space to run and play. It was like a giant treehouse.

His father was sitting cross-legged by the firepit, grinning and roasting a marshmallow. He waved his seven-year-old son over and handed him a stick, and they sat together and watched the fire lick at the little white pillows. The monkeys swung above them in the branches, paying them no attention. If he tried to look directly at them, they vanished. Only in his periphery could he see their shapes, and even then, not clearly.

"Great view, isn't it?" his father said.

They gazed at the twinkling city lights in the distance, listening to the cars honking on the freeways.

Caleb swallowed. "Are you—dead?"

His dad smiled. "Who knows? Does it really matter?" He slid his melted marshmallow off the stick and stuck it between two graham crackers topped with chocolate bars. There was a long silence as they ate. Then he said, "Tell me something, Caleb. Are you happy?"

"As much as anyone else, I guess."

"In my experience, most people are not happy. Do you know why?"

Caleb shook his head.

"It's because they lose all sense of the wonder of life. People get old and grow too much hair in their ears and they can't hear anything anymore. They've forgotten that life is a game, and that's all. It's supposed to be fun! Monkeys can steal a body—and hey, why not? You believed it once, and now here we are. Sometimes it's easy to forget who we really are, until we sit at the top of a tree with a monkey."

He thought as he finished chewing. He swallowed and snapped his fingers in realization. "You know why I think people forget that life's supposed to be fun? It's very simple. They become too serious, so much so that they feel like they must control life. They work out constantly, and take twenty-nine vitamins a day, and tend to their 401(k)s, and ruminate about how they don't want to be old and decrepit, so they must take care of themselves at all costs. They become afraid of everything that is uncontrolled, including other people.

"So it's very important that they control your life as much as they can. Or, at the least, they have to make sure you take life as seriously as they do. I'm sure you know many people like this. Life is miserable for them, so they have to make it miserable for you, too. If everyone's as angry and upset and tired as they are, then they feel like they're doing just fine.

"You know what they want more than anything, those people who tell you what you have to think and feel? Your attention and, most importantly, your time. That's what they really want. They are time thieves. They want to suck it away from you! It's the one thing no one can make more of, and they won't stop until what is yours is theirs.

"Stop giving yourself to your job. And to politicians. In fact, to all these so-called causes. They're sucking the life out of you. They can't be trusted. Neither can CEOs and presidents of large corporations, or the pope, or other authority figures. They already own all the land and the homes and the gold and the satellites—but they want more! They want your time and your attention and your energy. They can't settle for some—they want it all!

"I command you to refuse them! You have to play and have fun and get muddy, especially when things seem the darkest. I want you to smash your screens, and smash your friends' screens, and take your time back. The capitalists want your time, and the communists want it too! And the computer wants it, and your phone wants it. Fuck them! Fuck them all!"

The wind gusted hard and kicked up the flames, jettisoning burning yellow into the leaves and branches above. Soon the whole treetop was ablaze, and swinging back and forth in the heavy windstorm that had begun.

Ooh ooh aah aah—

Caleb and his father and the monkeys howled together as the treetop rocked back and forth. The trunk creaked and groaned, each bend lowering them closer to the earth before springing back the other direction.

His father looked over and the now forty-five-year-old Caleb grinned back at him, and the tree swung to and fro, and in the streets below, men and women gathered outside to watch the flaming top swinging like an upside-down pendulum, way back this way and way back that way, and then it arched closer and closer to the ground, and it whipped back, and the treetop tore from the trunk and sailed into the sky, over the horizon, only to become a pinpoint over the ocean before disappearing completely.

And if you look out of your window during one of the strange hours, when your mind is properly attenuated, you might glimpse a fiery fan palm frond sailing through the air, and you might hear the *ooh ooh aah aahs* of the monkeys within, and you might even join them if you're not too old and crusty and calcified to do so.

If it's too late for you, then be sure to tell your children.

Before it's too late for them, too.

The Floating Brain

PROLOGUE

OUT BEYOND THE CITIES BARELY BOUND BY TENUOUS threads of civilization, above the scorched lands, there hovered an improbable creature. Haunting the wasted Outerlands, it knew only how to roam—and consume.

Harnessing the energy of nuclear fallout, the brain emerged from the wreckage of man's demented wars. Goaded by the scientists, it grew large in the labs. Their experiments yielded something impossible: it floated off the ground, and took flight, eventually set loose to keep the peace outside the cities. No modern weapons—no rockets, no bullets, no atomic bombs—had ever penetrated its electromagnetic shield. It floated along its own path, unmolested. The exhausted population of what was left of North America had little choice but to accept the fact that to escape the cities meant almost certain death in the mouth of the giant floating brain.

Yet some did escape, and set up smaller societies of their own. They maintained a safe distance from the authorities; in turn, the government left them alone. But these rebels would not accept the floating brain that terrorized them. Living underground, they formulated a plan of attack many years in the making.

Some nights, they would hide outside, under a few scattered bushes, and gaze up at this monster, this freak of nature, as it floated in from the west. It had eyes, a slight semblance of a nose beneath, and a flapping mouth with no teeth. Its lips served merely as an entrance to the foul hole that swirled and churned with an acidic tongue.

It was a beastly thing. Yet it did have an intellect, and sensory tentacles that lowered two hundred feet to the floor of the earth. Through them, the brain sensed movement—and snatched up humans in a flash, flipping them into its cavernous mouth and swallowing them whole.

But its truly special intelligence, the one forged in the lab—its psychotronic energy—was the government's real achievement. The agent who nurtured it also possessed the gift that allowed him to communicate with the brain. Tethered to it, he could transmit messages through the "mind-pipe" that connected them.

For years it seemed as though the government and

the brain had won the war against the rebels. Until the day came for the rebels to instigate an attack of their own, when the government would least expect it. But just as the plan was to be executed, the agent Herod discovered a mole in his organization. Dean Kent, one of his most trusted scientists, had betrayed them.

This is the story of what happened, of how Kent's daughter, Ursula, would find herself thrust into battle, besieged by self-doubt and overwhelming responsibility, and of the psychotronic warfare between her, the agent Herod, and the floating brain. . . .

I

EVERY MAN DIES ALONE

THERE WAS NO POINT IN RUNNING. NO ONE HIS AGE COULD escape in less than twenty minutes. Not from his apartment, forty-three floors in the air, out into open territory with no mode of transportation.

Besides, Dean Kent was tired of running.

The officials of One-State, his employer for the last many decades, were coming. He wondered blankly what kind of weapons they would bring, and how many, and what devices they'd use first to get the answers they needed. He'd heard rumors before, of course: of who was taken, and why, and how, and what was done to them after.

He shook his head, trying to push the thoughts away. He wasn't going to change his mind about staying behind, not even with Ursula upset like she was.

The tears from his seventeen-year-old girl were

unaccompanied by emotion. Her face, blank, her eyes, nimble and calculating. Somewhere inside her were the feelings. She had an odd stoic look, a shell of a burgeoning lady, like a robot trapped inside a human body.

Though he'd always guessed that one day he'd have to say goodbye, the preparations hadn't made it any easier. They somehow made it worse. He only wished now he could stay behind and see her blossom into the woman he hoped he'd raised her to be.

Ursula cinched her pack tightly. She'd already packed it with the bare necessities, and minutes ago they'd filled it with the rest with the supplies she'd need for her journey. They'd cut the weight down to fifty pounds, fully loaded, which was too heavy but would have to do. There was no telling how long she'd be on the road or what she might encounter. Fortunately, she'd trained hard enough, and long enough, and could handle the weight.

She was tall for a young woman, just under six feet. In the old days, Dean thought, she'd be called a tomboy. For some reason he felt guilty about that. A single father, he'd raised her the only way he knew how, and if she was unladylike, well, that was his doing. The choices of parenthood—the hard, difficult, almost existential dilemmas he faced—he hoped he'd done enough to prepare her for what would come next.

He gazed upon her, and had to look away. I should have picked another career, he thought. Never should have gotten involved in this mess, the warfare, the psychicism, the goddamn floating brain. . . .

But those thoughts were pointless now. Whatever he would have done differently, it was too late for that.

Much too late.

"Please come with me," Ursula said. "We can do this together. Can't we?"

He shook his head and pulled her close. "I would only slow you down. This is too important. You are too important." He wiped the wetness from her cheek and pointed to a spot on the map that lay on the heavy oak table. "Here's your first destination."

"The park?"

"Yes. This spot here."

When he was satisfied she had committed the area to memory, Dean struck a match and lit the map on fire. It burned to ash in the garbage can.

He glanced at the clock. Sixteen minutes left.

"Get there and wait for a man named Remy. He'll take you the rest of the way."

"But where am I going?"

"It will be explained to you. Everything's been set up."

"I don't want to. I don't want to go."

He pulled her close. "Listen to me. I trained you to be a warrior. I've known this day would come and never told you the details, to protect you and the rebellion. There was no other way.

"When you get out of the city, you'll find different kinds of people. They're not going to understand you. They won't like you. It will be dangerous. You'll have to stay vigilant, all the time, the moment you step out this door."

"The people in the park, too?" she asked. "They're dangerous?"

"Yes. Them, the One-State officials, the rebels. And . . ."

"The brain?" Her eyes went wide.

He exhaled. "Yes. The brain. So you see, the whole world is about to become very vicious. You have something, a gift, that they want. It's buried deep inside you. The government wants it. The brain wants it. The rebels will want it, too.

"There's something you'll have to do with your gift. You'll have to give yourself over to it when you reach your destination. So you'll have to trust me when I tell you that all will be revealed to you, when the time is right."

He narrowed his eyes. "You remember your Hamlet?"

She nodded.

"Good. *'Conscience doth make cowards of us all.'* Remember that. That's the code. When Remy takes you to your final spot, the person assigned to help you will say that phrase. That's how you'll know they're legitimate."

"What am I going to do?"

"I can't tell you. You'll just have to trust me—and forgive me for not giving you the life you should have had."

He glanced at the clock. Fourteen minutes now.

"You're going to be late," he said. He pulled her in for one last hug. "You remember how to leave, right?"

She nodded.

"Good." He smiled gently and lingered on one last look. She reminded him so much of her mother, that same long red hair and deep green eyes. She even clenched her jaw and maintained the same intense stare when she was focusing.

"Don't come back," he said. "Don't ever come back."

She looked away, then spun around and rushed in for

one last hug.

He gave it to her as his heart pounded.

Then she was gone, and he was alone.

Dean waited until he could no longer hear her footfalls on the cheap linoleum flooring of the hallway before turning his mind to the next task.

Night would soon fall.

His window, facing west, bore the best views of the landscape during sundown. It wouldn't be long before the brain came. It always came from the west, every night. Many, many years before, going west meant hope, adventure, prosperity.

Now it meant only death.

A death he'd helped create.

He turned away and ran through his plan once more. Anything containing sensitive information about his work had been dumped or burned. There was nothing to suggest where Ursula would be going. Nothing that could tell the authorities, and that bastard Herod, what their plans were; how the rebels could try to kill, once and for all, that giant floating brain. That *thing*, that bastard son of science. God, there wasn't a day that went by that he wished he could rewind time.

But those were different times. The Blackout had taken everything from everybody; the entire country had had to rebuild from the ground up. He remembered as a young man the nights without electricity, the world gone dark, and how he had stared out into the woods, hearing the strange sounds of the wilderness that civilization had kept at bay for thousands of years, realizing that in a single instant they had been plunged back into darkness, all their progress erased. It was then that he knew what his life's work would be: to help restore the light, lest the human race face again that primal madness from which they had once escaped.

And out of those times, when everything had been a desperate grasping for restoration, came his work, and One-State, and the brain.

You used your daughter, a little voice inside him said. You're using her to atone for your sins. You've stolen her life from her. Now she will never be free to live a normal one. Because of you and what you did. Because you had to raise her to fix things. You never gave her the chance to choose what to do and how to live. She's only living now to help *you*.

And she doesn't even know.

He felt the tears coming and he didn't stop them. There was nothing else to be done. He checked the wastebasket to make sure the map had burned, confirming also that he'd destroyed all the evidence he'd had. He'd sent his robo-man assistant, Ditsch, away, to hide himself at a trusted friend's home. He couldn't bring himself to decommission his close friend of the last ten years.

Which left Dean himself as the last remaining source of information.

Eight minutes now.

He slowly circumvented the apartment, taking in all the memories one last time. They'd lived here twenty years, in the same apartment, he and Ursula, and his wife, once, before she died.

So absorbed in his thoughts, he almost didn't notice the flashing lights of the drone copters.

They're early, he thought. He was a high-profile target; they probably expedited their response times just for him.

He backed away from the window. He would have liked to tell Herod to his face what he'd been planning for so long, shortly after they had completed the experiments in the human amygdala that allowed them to—

Enough.

It was time to get on with it.

After barricading the front door, to slow them down a few extra minutes, Dean opened the veins in his arms with the serrated knife. For good measure, he sliced the femoral artery in his left leg.

He may have felt nothing but guilt for many years, but in his last moments, as his vision swam gray, he knew he'd done at least one thing right: raise and train a woman who might one day win her freedom.

Somehow, in those final moments, that outweighed all else he'd done.

It would have to.

2

Ursula Runs

Ursula's mind, only seconds ago a jumbled mess of thoughts and feelings, cleared as the elevator took her down. Here she was, after years of preparation, with her pack fully loaded, about to be delivered into the wide open world. Her whole life had been leading up to this one mission, whatever it would turn out to be. She decided it was the feeling an ancient explorer might have:

when the boat was full and the men were stationed, just before pushing off onto the sea.

The door opened. She crossed into the hallway, her flex but rugged boots squeaking on the cheap flooring. Bits of a broken light bulb crunched underfoot as she pushed open the exit door and stepped out onto the dirt field, passing the lone pole with a badly sun-scorched tetherball attached to a decaying rope—the one she'd used as a young girl.

She glanced back once at the building where she'd spent her life, muttered a quick goodbye, then began jogging, hooking north until she passed through a copse of trees and turned west. Picking up speed down the trail, she pressed on, feeling her excitement, willing her breath to steady so she could maintain a good pace. After a minute or so she found her rhythm, and soon she was far enough away that she didn't even hear the sirens of the drone-copter as they arrived to arrest her father.

THE PARK WAS FULL OF DRUGS AND VIOLENCE, AND NOT much else. Girls like her did not come to places like this. She had known only one teen, a rough-and-tumble rebel named Claire, who had decided to venture out to score some animal on a dare from her friends. No one heard from her again. It was one of those stories parents told their kids: *Don't do drugs like Claire did. They'll make you crazy, and then you'll go into the woods and never come out.*

She checked her watch as she crossed the aging bridge that stretched over a dead stream, following the path her father had outlined to her. She knew it by heart, the exact mileage from each trail to the next, divided by paces. Counting her steps was second nature now.

The wind-chill of the unfurling night made her

shiver through her sweat. Without stopping, she hooked an arm behind her pack, snagged the wool scarf her mother had knitted her long ago, and wrapped it around her neck in a fluid motion.

Pleased with her breathing, she pressed on. It was measured and controlled, just like she'd trained for. She could go five miles at a two-third sprint with her pack, if she needed to.

Somewhere up in the thirty-foot sycamore trees overhead, an owl hooted. She hooted back and grinned, glancing upward at the treetops but seeing nothing. The owl was hiding. That was good. They had something in common. She felt as though she'd made a friend.

Cresting over the rising dirt path, she turned right and passed a small clearing some fifty feet off-trail. Slowing, she caught her breath and looked around. The sun had disappeared, but the moon was yet to rise.

She pushed through the next wall of pine tree branches on the opposite side of the clearing until she found the giant rock. Here she would wait for Remy. It had only taken her an hour. She unclipped her pack and crouched with her back to the rock.

Now there was nothing to do but wait.

As her heart thumped, her hand instinctively gripped the handle of the six-inch knife on her belt below the small of her back. The crouching would help keep her in a readied position in case of attack. Her father had taught her to rely on instinct, that if something seemed amiss it probably was. In the forest that partly meant letting your eyes scan for anything horizontal. Things tended to grow up, not sideways, and if she saw a lumpy or prone shape, it could indicate something human.

But she saw nothing. When she felt safe, she let her

thoughts compile any other useful information about her surroundings and what to do in case of a surprise attack from this direction or that. The mind, her father had said, can pre-process almost anything, and many people panic and die in a tough situation because of a kind of expectation-shock: that reality was not what they thought it would be. So the trick was to expect nothing but prepare for anything.

She stood, relieving her knees, when she heard a stick snap somewhere above.

She looked up and froze.

Three misshapen figures, pale, hunching and gnarled, kneeling on the rock above, reached down to grab her.

3

HEROD CUTS

I'VE BEEN DOING THIS TOO LONG, HEROD THOUGHT.

It was the screams that were doing him in. They triggered his migraines and set his teeth grating, igniting his anger and clouding his judgment. He preemptively chewed an aspirin, hoping this time that torturing the robot would produce no noise at all.

Setting his poker face, he turned to address the being known as Ditsch, tied into a chair. He dangled a blade in front of the robo-man's face and motioned around the apartment of Dean Kent, the man whose body now lay in plastic wrap by the door.

It hadn't taken Herod long to find the robo-man; he'd rightly assumed that Dean couldn't bring himself to decommission his longtime assistant. So he'd sent an agent to grab Ditsch and bring him back to his master's apartment, his suspicion that the sight of the body might help produce the synthetic fear in the robot that Herod desired.

"It's a conundrum," he said. "On the one hand, I know you were built to never feel pain. But I also know your programming demands you protect your body, for you understand how it functions.

"So what I'm going to do is this. Better to tell you, in plain English, since you can understand basic facts." He sneered. "Even though you are no better emotionally than a primate."

"I speak hundreds of languages," the robo-man said blankly. Then he added: "Emotions are a language, too, you know."

"We'll see."

Herod stood behind the robo-man, facing the back of his head. Inserting the scalpel just below the occipital lobe, he cut downward until he reached the top of the acrylic spine, exposing the nano-wires.

"Can you feel me pulling gently on your wires?" Herod said. "Can you?"

"Yes," said the robo-man, his eyes wide, his face expressionless.

"You'll answer the questions I have about Dean Kent, and your work together, and the location of his daughter, and if I'm not satisfied with your answer, I'll cut every wire, one by one, until your motherboard dies."

"I'm not sure I can tell you what you want to know."

"You worked with him for twelve years. You were his assistant. I'm sure you know plenty."

Silence.

"Before we start, tell me, what are the odds I cut the wire powering your synthetic cortex? What are the chances I destroy your ability to reason?"

"One in 5,637."

"And if I cut one hundred at a time..."

"One in 56.37, rounded up to 57."

Herod cut a small handful of wires. A tiny wisp of smoke drifted from the torn connection.

"How many was that?" he asked. "I'm afraid I don't have the patience to count myself."

"Ninety-seven."

Was that a flicker of fear Herod saw in the eye of the robo-man? Ditsch had the same vacant stare he always did, but perhaps there was more to him than met the eye. He was, after all, shockingly human in many ways.

"The fact that you can talk," Herod said, "tells me I haven't crippled your cerebral circuits. Tell me, Ditsch, what *has* been affected?"

"My short-term random access memory has been disrupted."

"Which means converting new stimuli to long-term storage will be more difficult."

"Yes."

"Good. That means you still know what I want to know. I'll be straight with you, since I don't have enough time to let the techs dismantle you bit by bit. If you answer me, I won't have you completely destroyed. You may still be able to live the rest of your life serving One-State as a butler. Though I have to admit, I'd much rather see you a twisted hunk of silicone on the floor.

"Tell me, what was my old partner's plan? And where did he hide his daughter Ursula?"

"I'm afraid I don't know that."

"Which part don't you know?"

Silence.

Herod could almost see the wheels spinning in the robo-man's head.

"My memory is hazy. You must have cut the wrong wires after all."

Herod wasted no time. He dropped the scalpel and yanked a handful of wires from the robo-man's spine. The effect was immediate. Ditsch stiffened, then looked down slowly at his arms and legs. If he were human, the expression on his face might be one of stunned disbelief.

"Your stupidity surprises even me," Herod said. He unlocked the handcuffs around the robo-man's wrists and ankles, which had just been rendered useless. "We don't need these now. Anyway, I know you lie. I know for a fact that I never came close to damaging your long-term memory storage—those wires run inches deep into the center of your chest. Your creator saw fit to put them in place of a human heart, which I find oddly compassionate, don't you?

"The fact that you lied tells me that you understand the concept of self-preservation quite well. Nothing would give me more pleasure than to rid this world of your entire stinking race, and one day I might get that chance. For now I will settle on torturing you one wire at a time. Let me tell you how it will all happen."

Herod went on to describe the exact torture and method, and something like fear shot through the robo-man. Although it seemed impossible for him to make emotional decisions, the former assistant of Dean Kent was programmed to make rational ones, to save himself, and it was this mechanism that Herod exploited, learning, in the end, the first stop of Dean's daughter,

Ursula.

When Herod was satisfied, he tore the rest of the wires from Ditsch's neck, then stabbed his scalpel through the middle of the chest, tearing the synthetic flesh wide open. When he saw the light go out in the robo-man's eyes, he knew he had severed anything and everything that connected the robot to the likeness of man.

Herod stood and stretched his back. He felt much better. There had been no screaming this time. His migraine was lifting. He went to go find the girl.

4
Lost Boys

THE ONE IN THE MIDDLE CALLED RUNT HAD REACHED down to tap the girl on the shoulder and get her attention, when there was a sudden flash of a blade. He looked down to find two of his fingers in the dirt.

Ursula dropped into a combat stance, knees slightly bent, knife raised.

"Whoa, we're friends!" shouted one of them.

The figure on the left raised his hands. "I'm coming down now, Ursula. Don't come at me with that knife." He hopped off the rock. "My name's William."

Ursula backed up, still wielding her weapon. "How do you know my name?"

"Remy. Remy sent me, okay?"

In the moonlight streaming down through the foliage, Ursula could make out the face of a boy who couldn't have been much older than she. His clothes were nicer than the others'. He had high cheekbones with a raised scar that ran lengthwise down his face. She decided he was nice-looking, even with the scar, and he had a nice build she found pleasing. He must be the leader.

"Where's Remy?"

"He's at the safe house nearby."

"Why didn't he come himself?"

"He's hung up. Gathering supplies. For you."

Behind William, the other two cautiously approached.

They looked pitiful, ragged. Runt blubbered as he wrapped his stubs in a grimy piece of cloth. The other one, called Harmon, struggled to breathe through clogged nostrils. She felt nauseous and almost had to look away; no doubt he was one of the unlucky sufferers of "nose rot," a side effect of the artificial clouds. It infected the nasal pathways and caused the victim to produce quantities of bright green snot.

They're outcasts, she thought . . . but so are you.

"Okay," she said. "Take me to Remy. But you lead the way. Stay in front of me."

TEN MINUTES LATER, THEY REACHED A SMALL CLEARING at the base of a gentle hill. To their left was a wall of branches and leaves. William approached the wall and with a sweep of his hand folded back the ghillie net, exposing a makeshift shelter.

The shelter's walls were made from old, rusty tin paneling set against a wooden frame. The structure seemed to stretch far back, much deeper than she would have thought.

"Go ahead." William gestured inside.

The one with the missing fingers averted Ursula's

gaze, ashamed and embarrassed by his new deformity.

"And don't worry about Runt," William said. "He'll be fine once he gets a little animal in him."

Runt perked up, the pain in his hand seemingly vanished. "You - you got animal?"

"Of course I do. Not too much now though, ya hear?" He winked at Ursula and removed a vial containing a brown powder from his ratty coat pocket.

Runt's eyes lit up. In a flash, he pulled a metal tube from his back pocket. Setting one end of the tube into the vial, he jammed the other into his nose for a good snort.

Almost immediately his shoulders slumped. A goofy grin fanned across his face. His eyes glazed over. He stumbled off a few feet and plopped in the dirt, appearing disoriented but not seeming to care.

William shrugged at Ursula and grinned. It made her uneasy. She hadn't pegged him as a drug user. She wondered what else she might be wrong about. It disquieted her.

Ursula waved the boys aside and scooted the metal door open enough for her to let herself in. Then she pulled it shut behind her.

She entered a hallway roughly twenty feet long, the walls made of the same corrugated metal as the exterior. Small candles, lit, were mounted, providing some light. Squinting, she saw the flicker of something like a larger fire at the end of the hall.

She moved toward the flickering and turned right. The tunnel in that direction ended after ten feet. She found herself in a living space containing a small bed, some wooden bookshelves, and a chest for clothes. It was remarkably clean for a shanty; all the outdoor people she'd seen in the past had a hard time keeping their spaces so neat.

"Remy? It's Ursula Kent!"

She stepped into the next room. A man with long brown hair tied into braids was sitting in a rocking chair, facing away. Next to him, a boiling pot hung over a small fire. The stew inside bubbled fiercely.

"Remy?" she said again, placing a hand on the man's shoulder.

Remy Lazardo toppled over into the fire, clanging his head on the metal pot. As he fell, his body twisted around, and Ursula glimpsed the hole in his chest.

She froze. Only for a split second.

But even that was too much.

A hand wrapped around her mouth from behind. Another set of hands snatched the knife before wrestling her to the floor.

She kicked and screamed, muffled, through the fingers that smelled like dirt and blood. She felt grit in her teeth. Bucking as hard as she could, she whipped her legs up, trying to get some space between her back and the man holding her. But it was no use.

William and the third one, Harmon, tried to take her to the floor.

Runt crouched in the corner, lolling his tongue. His face appeared lopsided in the fire-shadow; his blank stare courtesy of the animal in his bloodstream made him look all the more terrifying. He got up and staggered, nearly pitching headfirst into the fire alongside Remy, whose scorched body was already beginning to stink.

Ursula soon found herself overpowered and stopped fighting. Better to save her strength and wait for the right moment. She could get out of this, but she had to be smart. If they'd wanted her dead, they would have killed her by now.

"We wait here." William caught his breath, arms wrapped around her from behind. "And you be good."

"Will we get paid?" Runt asked.

"Oh, we'll get paid. This one's worth good money to Herod, I'm sure." William turned to Ursula, his hot, rancid breath steaming on her face. "We knew Remy was up to something. We got it out of him, though. Said he was taking you to the Barrows. City girl like you, gotta be up to no good. We keep an eye on these things for Herod."

"We'll get more animal—and be free!" cackled Runt, who was now rifling through every inch of the place looking for something to steal.

Ursula stayed silent. Feigning surrender, she let her arms go limp, which had the desired effect of both boys loosening their grip on her arms and waist—just a little —providing some wiggle room.

Now it was a matter of not panicking.

The Barrows, he'd said. The forest. That's where she was to go. If she made it out of here, of course. The thought of traveling that far from the city, through the wasteland, in the realm of the brain . . . her stomach sank at the thought. She'd never seen the Barrows, never thought she'd ever see them. She only knew the direction in which to walk.

And this Herod he mentioned . . . she recognized the name. Someone her father worked with, maybe? She couldn't place it. But there was little time for that now. It made no difference who was coming for her, only that someone was coming. So she focused on calming herself, on letting the adrenaline dissipate.

Harmon let her go to take a snort of animal, and Runt took more as well, and then William decided to have some too, and as Harmon halfway stumbled back over to hold her so William could have another fill, Ursula felt no hands on her at all for a split second, and it was then that she sprang into action.

She went for the vial of animal first, knocking it to the floor, guessing correctly that Harmon would instinctively reach for it before her. And he did. In the half-second of confusion it produced, she kicked the pot of boiling stew into his face.

Ursula caught wisps of each image, as in a photograph. The pot swinging in the air. The hiss of the stew sizzling on wasted flesh. The roar of the maimed man and the rage of his blind fury. Later she would vaguely recall pulling her blade from William's holster, the one he'd confiscated from her, then turning to the one called Runt and chasing him down—her snarls seeming to take physical shape—then the flashing of the blade, the red from his wound, and the whimpering sounds.

William bolted. Harmon's face was a bubbling mess. As grotesque he was, and as sorry she might have felt for him under different circumstances, the situation was what it was. She couldn't have any of them following her. She grabbed her pack, strapped it on and cinched it tight, then in one swipe cut the exposed Achilles tendon on Harmon's right ankle.

She did not allow herself to hear the screams.

5
WORLD WAR IV

THE ROADS, IF YOU COULD CALL THEM THAT, OUT OF THE park and into the Outerlands, consisted of fifty miles of alternating scorched earth and random groves of frail trees one windstorm away from tipping over.

Many had predicted long ago that World War III would wipe out most of the inhabitable earth. In fact, it was World War IV that did it, as much due to the artificial intelligence and electromagnetic weapons as the atom bombs.

The electromagnetics were originally designed to be used sparingly, to take out electricity and the internet, only at key points along an enemy's axis, but the tactic had quickly spiraled out of control. What resulted was a logistical nightmare of crumpled factories, broken supply chains, and labor shortages. There was simply no economy left. Communication quickly broke down. Nothing seemed to work. Governments locked down their energy supplies, halting exports and sending food prices skyrocketing.

All of which eventually led to a hot war between the nations.

Only seven nukes were dropped, but that had been enough. San Francisco had been wiped out entirely, splattered like a bug under a boot. The trade winds blowing south carried radiation across the southwest, poisoning a hundred million Americans. Other bombs were dropped on Tehran, Beijing, Moscow, Colorado, and New York City.

The worst fallout, however, came from the hundreds

of nuclear power plants around the world. Unable to retain a staff, many facilities simply melted down before they could be decommissioned. In fact, everything west of Idaho and down to Arizona, and everything east from Ohio to Alabama, was considered uninhabitable.

Dean Kent had insisted on teaching his daughter the country's history, from its founding until the present. Sometimes he would grow quiet and wistful and spend the night at the window, watching the dim outline of the brain as it stalked the skies in the distance. His moods made her turn quiet and inward as well; her knowledge of the world had always been filtered through him.

Until now.

URSULA EMERGED FROM THE PARK FOREST INTO THE Outerlands and stretched her legs as she gazed into the wide, dusty expanse. Somewhere, the brain was roaming. As scared as she was to have to brave its territory, she was desperate to put as much distance between herself and the park as she could. By her estimation she might be able to reach the Barrows by sunup, if she hurried.

There was nothing else to do except start trudging.

6

HEROD CONTACTS THE BRAIN

HEROD ALWAYS TRIED TO AVOID WORKING WITH THOSE HE despised, and that included druggers like the three who had killed Remy. Their single-minded focus on staying high was useful and distracting at the same time: he could rely on them to do whatever was needed to get their next fix, but anything beyond that risked derailing the task at hand.

Their miserable crew, however, had discovered one useful piece of information that made the fiasco worthwhile. Ursula would be headed to the Barrows, an oasis of forest west of the city. She'd have to pass through the Outerlands, that barren stretch of cracked clay over which the brain presided. And she'd be on foot.

Herod could only guess what she knew. His instincts told him she likely wasn't aware of any larger plan. Her father had always been careful, keeping people on a need-to-know basis. Herod surmised it was no different this time. To protect her, Dean wouldn't have told her much.

He chomped on another aspirin. Placing the bottle into his coat pocket, he sighed and got to work on making contact with the brain.

HEROD HAD HIS AGENTS CLEAR A THREE-HUNDRED-FOOT circle around the shelter. Privacy was vital now, and too many park people had begun to gather.

He sank to his knees outside the shelter, removing his black cowboy hat and the bandanna wrapped around his forehead. He felt the raised flesh there, in the center of his forehead, directly above the space between the eyes.

It wasn't a scar.

His fingernail grasped an edge of the raised flesh. Pulling the skin up until he could hook a thumb under, he peeled it back the rest of the way. There was no blood.

The hole in his head was about the size of a walnut. It was dark in there, but if you had a flashlight, you could see the thing—the third eye—pulsing inside.

He rotated his body west, in the direction of the brain, and raised his head to the sky. The artificial clouds had dissipated by then; a stream of moonlight through the trees shone upon the eye in its dark cavern. It pushed itself forward, protruding from his skull, basking in the soft glow.

His process of connecting with the brain was always the same. Dissociation, at first. A gentle unmooring from the physical world around him, before it faded away altogether.

His jaw fell open as he muttered something unintelligible. He fell back on his knees, his legs folding under him. Somewhere within and without himself he saw the round top of the mind-pipe flying toward him from the heavens. It connected, ramrodding into the front of his skull, a length of stiff metal with no give. The other end gyrated madly, jerking him. The invisible rod from the sky seemed to screw tighter into his head, with tension. The pressure mounted. Intense pressure. His third eye pulsed. The sensation pleased him.

His neck stretched. Tendons creaked as he was pulled to all fours like a dog. His face grew thick with blood rushing from his extremities into his chest, neck, and head.

The third eye needed the blood.

The suction in his head grew more intense. The eye felt as if it were about to burst. As always, just when he could stand it no longer, when he was sure his brains would be sucked out of the hole, there was a sudden pop, and he felt an instant release.

He collapsed and caught his breath, letting himself settle into his new vision. It wasn't vision in the visual sense. It was more like a vague, swirling shape of things inside his head. An approximation of internal vision, with no sound. This was a sixth sense, unlike the other five.

Presently he could "see" the mind-pipe in fuzzy greens and blues stretching from his head into the ether beyond the park. The colors shifted and coalesced, until he could make out a faint gray blob at the other end.

He and the floating brain were connected.

This would last for only a few moments. But that was more than enough time for Herod to send all the information he needed to, to let the brain know where he thought Ursula would be and what to do with her when she was found.

Ursula's throat throbbed and head pounded.

The air out here was dirty and dusty and mean. She would have to conserve what little water she had. She cursed herself for not bringing more. The morning light would soon be upon her; she guessed she only had another hour of darkness. She would rest when it got too hot during the day. But right now she needed to move.

Up ahead she saw a drop-off, a hill sloping down into a bowl. Beyond the bowl was the Barrows, the patch of forest with enough cover for her to rest and contemplate her next move.

If she could make it there.

Halfway down the ravine, she was watching the ground, minding her steps to avoid any pitfalls, when a shadow washed over her shoes.

She looked up and stopped suddenly, sending loose rocks tumbling down the ravine.

A hundred feet off the ravine floor, the brain hovered.

She froze, able only to gawk at its gray, bulbous mass. Those flaps and folds of the membrane, wet and sticky with slime that dripped on the ground and sizzled when it hit. Its tentacles, dragging along the dirt. Ursula remembered what her father had told her: that the tentacles sensed movement through vibrations in the earth.

It secreted several types of oozes, scientists had discovered. One paralyzed the victim outright; another acted like a drug that disrupted one's sense of time and space, producing complete terror and an overwhelming compulsion to be in open air. Anything enclosed felt unbearably claustrophobic. Upon rushing out of their hiding place, the person would be face-to-face with the brain.

Another type of ooze was like acid, burning straight through anything it touched.

Ursula watched, hardly breathing, as the brain hung spookily in the air. When it drifted along, it did so silently and without using its tentacles for support.

One of the initial mysteries about the brain was how exactly it floated. Scientists had discovered its talent in the lab, but had never cracked its secrets. Their best guess was that it harvested radioactive isotopes from spent nuclear particles, and as it grew it figured out how to harness them as an antigravity force. It was some kind of evolution that humans could not understand, proven by their hundreds of failed attempts at reproducing its antigravity.

So absorbed was she in watching the brain that she didn't register the bighorn sheep approaching not one hundred feet to her right. Running up the side of the bowl, it kicked some rocks; they noisily tumbled down the ravine.

She froze.

In an instant, the brain jettisoned itself, reaching the sheep in mere seconds.

Its tentacle snatched the animal up, flipping it into its mouth. Bawling and screeching, the sheep was swallowed whole. The brain had no teeth, just a slimy cavernous hole with tubular striations on the inside like tiny razors that stripped the hair, gristle, and flesh off the bones of its victims.

A glop of spittle fell on a cactus nearby. The plant sizzled. Ursula stifled a cough, her nostrils burning from the toxic smoke. Through her fingers, she felt blood trickling from her nose.

The brain's digestion of the sheep was loud and wet. Ursula laid on her side, daring not even to glance up. All around her, tentacles fell. The brain hovered, floating almost directly above her, waiting for any other movement in her vicinity it could detect sympathetically through the ground.

It seemed to know she—or something—was there.

In fact, it did know. That was the message sent psychically from Herod. To the brain, the message arrived in the form of hazy images. It meant to find her.

It was very important that it find her. The man had told it so.

TEN MINUTES LATER, THE BRAIN WAS STILL HOVERING above. Bits of slime dripped all around, missing her by inches.

She rested her cheek on the dirt. She gripped her bleeding nose with two fingers and mouth-breathed.

Nothing happened for several more minutes.

Then, something did.

The dirt began to move, to her left, as if the rocky

floor were alive.

The thing the size of a fist, four or five feet away, emerged from the dirt. It scurried on eight legs. Ursula fought the urge to scream as the tarantula reached full size.

Still, she didn't move. A venomous spider bite she might survive. The brain, she would not.

It crawled closer.

She closed her eyes, hoping it would ignore or miss her.

When it was one foot away—*whap!*—a tentacle snatched it up, whipping it back to the brain's mouth, where it disappeared.

A bit of goo from the tentacle landed on Ursula's arm. It sizzled, burning a hole the size of a penny. That singular, drilling pain—*Did it hit bone? Did it hit bone?* Her mind cried out in panic.

Her arm jerked. It happened automatically. It was unconscious and reactive, a spontaneous move.

But one move was all it took.

The brain's tentacles stopped searching. Everything went still. Ursula looked up. The brain seemed to rotate downward, on a central axis. Its face, if you could call it that, leered down at her. It had something resembling two eyes, and a nose, a grody and nauseating indentation amid the folds of membrane. The mouth twisted and opened. Its tongue fell. It had found its target.

When a blast rocked the brain from behind. Fire erupted in a halo around its protective shield, knocking it from its comfy perch in the sky, sending it spinning to the left. It was unharmed, but furious.

Ursula looked. A small plume of smoke rose at the wood's edge.

Someone had fired a rocket.

The brain regained its balance and, roaring now, zoomed toward the forest. In a few seconds, it was already beating the treetops with its tentacles, spraying venom, frantically searching for the culprit.

With precious seconds to spare, Ursula leapt to her feet and sprinted to the right side of the rocky slope. She'd climb over the lip of the slope and find someplace to hide. All she knew now was that she had to escape, and fast.

A few steps in, however, she began to sway. Dizziness swept over her as the brain's poison spittle took effect.

Her legs gave way first. She toppled forward.

Her last memory was of a hazy form bounding over the rocks toward her and the feeling of weightlessness that followed.

7

THE MIND-PIPE BURSTS

HEROD FOUND HIMSELF FLYING BACKWARD AS THE ROCKET blast hit. He saw, in his third eye, the mind-pipe bend and snap as if a bomb concealed inside had exploded. The world twisted beneath and around him, and then he landed on the dirt some twenty feet away.

His third eye vibrated in shock, pain, fury. He screamed, desperately trying to wedge two fingers into the hole to prevent the eye from backing deeper into his brain. His head felt like tackle boxes full of gear clanking heavily down the stairs. Searing, white-hot starbursts exploded inside his skull.

He fell face first onto the ground, fingernails drawing blood as they scrabbled for space between the eye and his soft tissue. This had happened only once before, seven years earlier, when he'd been psychically locked in with a Chinese diplomat as a hydro bomb exploded on the other end of their communications. The violence done to his brain was so great it took two weeks for him to hear properly, and another two weeks of blindness before recovering from the detached retinas. That time, his third eye had burrowed so far inside his head that the pressure had burst a blood vessel and nearly killed him.

This was an emergency. Right now he had to triage the situation by keeping the eye away from the back of his brain. He dug his fingers in deeper and felt around until he touched its squishy backside. It was indeed turned around, facing backward.

The eye squealed in protest, sliding every which way to circumvent the fingers.

Herod could feel it trembling.

Oh, God. No.

It was preparing to fire a torrent of energy, straight to Herod's brain. Kill the host, that's what would happen now, unless—

Turn it around! Turn it around!

Then a voice rang out somewhere close. Herod barely registered it.

William stumbled into the small clearing as Herod spun the eye around to face front.

The iris swelled and unleashed its energy.

William's head exploded into a fine powder. The snap of his neck from the psychic force tore his spine clean out of his body and landed fifteen feet away. The rest of him fell in a crumpled heap, a raggedy mix of skin, organs, and loosely connected bones.

The eye let loose a volley of energetic bursts. Herod could only try to wrangle his head in a general direction.

He was spun around. Remy's shelter blew apart, the walls flying a dozen yards in the air. One corrugated edge caught a maple tree, burying itself inches deep.

Slowly the pulses became less frequent, and shallower. The energy pumps quickened again, briefly, then stopped for good.

The eye had tired itself out.

It settled.

And went to sleep.

Herod sank to his knees and vomited. There was blood in it. His quick thinking had spun the eye, avoiding the worst outcome, but he knew it would be several days before he'd be able to see or hear a thing.

This time, he planned to sleep all the way through.

8

A Hell of Hallways

THE YEARS OF HER FATHER'S TRAINING HAD NOT BEEN easy.

Up at 5:00 a.m., six days a week. On Sundays she was allowed to sleep until six. After waking it was straight to brushing teeth, combing hair, and the ice bath. Four minutes in, one minute out. Two more minutes in, then to the shower.

Meditation followed, twenty minutes. The most important part of her routine. Then breakfast. An hour after waking she was ready to start the day.

Writing in the morning, mathematics, then history. She had no impulse to play like normal kids. She simply went about her business.

After lunch, she exercised her memory and mental strength. Sequencing training consisted of memorizing ten-digit strings of numbers, in sets of five. An hour of free time was next, usually from three to four in the afternoon. Sometimes she napped. Other times she played outside, but almost never with friends.

Dean would arrive home around four or five. Before dinner on Tuesdays, Thursdays, and Saturdays, he would train her. At first she studied aikido, then moved on to shotokan and jiu-jitsu. Mondays and Wednesday evenings were for strength training with free weights and a small leg-press machine.

A simple mindset—"no failure, only knowledge"—produced a clear mind. This focus came in handy during physical confrontations. She knew that her body's adrenaline response was involuntary, that it was important to separate the physical sensations from her mental state. Space between the two paradoxically translated into faster reflex time and the ability to respond instead of react.

Keeping her head about her was the best advantage she had.

When she awoke under the bright lights, it took her a moment to spatially map her surroundings. She blinked. Someone was standing slightly above her, to her right. A man. He was distracted, and facing away.

She glanced left. Seeing no one, she went into action, leaping up and shoving him from behind. He stumbled, wide-eyed, and yelped as he careened into the wall.

In the few seconds it took to reach the door, she clocked the all-white room she was in. Some kind of padding lined the walls. Finding the door locked, she whipped around in time to register the man lurching to his feet, snarling and rushing at her. Pivoting, Ursula swung her leg in a roundhouse, connecting her heel to his head. With a cry he went down, and then he was still. She grabbed his keys from the chain on his belt. Slid them into the lock until one clicked. Yanked the door open and ran into the—

Hallway. She was in a gray hallway with no windows, only heavy doors lining either side. Nothing to suggest what these rooms were, where she was, or how to get out. Choosing a direction, she ran.

Where was she? Who had brought her here? And why?

No time for all that.

Survival first. Questions later.

She focused her breathing. She sprinted on, trying to determine where she was. Yellow lights flickered above her head every twenty feet or so. Wooden beam reinforcements traced the sides of the hallway, from the floor to the ceiling.

Of course. With the brain above, bunkers were the only way to steer clear and live a normal life in the Outerlands. She must be somewhere underground.

She examined the keys. Maybe twenty of them on the chain. Who knew which went to which door.

Running on now. Soon the man she'd knocked out would wake up, or someone else would find her. She didn't like being cornered, and this hallway was too small for comfort to fight multiple opponents. She needed to find space, and fast.

She tried the next two doors to her right, but found

no key that fit. At the third door she felt the satisfying give of the lock, and the key turned, and she let out a little cry of joy, and then she barged in.

Two steps in she reared back, gasping, choking off a scream as the distorted heads stared back at her. Human heads. Animal heads. Dozens of them, all floating in vats of green, translucent liquid.

A three-eyed male, its head swollen and distended to twice its normal size, with tendrils of skin and membrane trailing from its shredded neck, tilted to one side, as if to say, "What are you doing here?"

She trembled at the half-pigs on display across the room, and at the skinless horse in a gigantic plastic dome, its veins and arteries and capillaries on full display.

Test-tube experiments, every one, preserved in amber liquid.

Of course, since she was a child she'd heard about the radioactive mutations, the spontaneous growths and chromosomal damage that bio-accumulated up the food chain or passed to the offspring of affected humans and animals. She turned and nearly sank to her knees as she saw the people with flippers for arms. Their bodies, resembling bloated seals, floated in massive vats. Congealed fat, white and hard, stretched from their chests to below their hips in one long runway around their lightbulb-shaped torsos.

And their feet. Their little flipper feet, with little webbed toes.

Their eyes glimmered, the gulf between the innocence in their faces and their horrific bodies widening with each moment she bore witness.

Did every room along the hallway contain these

oddities? Anyone who would run this freak show must have plans for her, too. Would they chop her up and fill her lungs with the green stuff? Expose her to radiation and let it run rampant inside her?

No.

NO.

Get out. She had to get out.

She sprinted out the door. Must get away. Anywhere but here—

Slamming blindly into something, she spun and wheeled wildly. Her legs twisted up as she fell. She caught a glimpse of the figure in a black trench coat, jumbled images of long, black hair, and then she felt the figure wrap its arms around her in a bear hug.

Ursula heard a woman scream something about not wanting to hurt her, but she couldn't be sure and why were they holding her, and she had to get out.

Struggling, she yelled and tore herself away, throwing elbows and stomping feet. Ursula felt the satisfying crunch of toes beneath her heel. The woman howled and for a moment Ursula was free.

But her freedom was short-lived. The woman reached a lucky hand out and caught her by the hair, wrenching her backward to the floor. Then came the grappling hook, and all the woman had to do was wait for Ursula to tire out.

Eventually, she did. Ursula felt herself growing tired, the sleeper hold taking its effect.

Ursula would later recall the world turning fuzzy-gray, and then—oblivion.

9
CUTTER EXPLAINS

'CONSCIENCE DOTH MAKE COWARDS OF US ALL.'

The woman in the black trench coat, named Cutter, had repeated the phrase to Ursula when she woke up. It had taken a few minutes to settle Ursula down; she'd been in fighting mode, even after receiving the key phrase.

Cutter had never seen a young girl so feisty. She didn't seem to care about her wild, knotted hair, the dirt, or her god-awful smell. She refused to bathe until Cutter reminded her that keeping oneself clean helps keep a clean mind and makes one a better fighter.

They sat now in the kitchen of the laboratory, eating dinner. Ursula wore no restraints. There was no need to keep any oafish men as muscle. On the other side of the room, the cooks prepared dinner for the scientists and workers of the underground facility.

"We knew you were heading to the Barrows, so we stationed men at the forest line to intercept you," Cutter explained. "The brain got there before you did. It was our men who shot at it and gave you enough time to escape."

Ursula chewed her beans.

"But the poison had started to work on you. You were losing motor function. Luckily, we had a bead on you the moment you started running back up the ravine."

"Where are we now?"

"In an underground city, about four miles north of the Barrows."

"I'd like a room."

"That's fine. We have one for you."

For the first time Ursula looked her new companion

in the eye. Cutter looked about forty. She had shiny hair, strong eyebrows, and a serious look, like she carried something dark and heavy inside. Ursula could feel the weight of it. Like herself, this was not a woman who liked to take orders.

Ursula set her fork down. "Why am I here?"

"You mean, you don't know?"

Ursula shook her head.

"So it's true. Dean really does keep everything secret."

"Did."

"Excuse me?"

"He *did* keep everything secret."

"He's gone?"

Ursula nodded.

"Oh." Cutter took this in. "I'm sorry. He was a good man." She looked to Ursula for a sign of emotion. She saw nothing. Apparently Ursula's grieving was finished. "Why don't we get you to your room then? It's a bit of a walk."

Without hesitation, Ursula grabbed her bag.

THE CITY SQUARE, IF ONE COULD CALL IT THAT, WAS A wide-open underground space some fifty feet tall from floor to ceiling, and hundreds of feet in diameter. Makeshift pagodas and tables lined the perimeter. Buyers and sellers streamed every which way—it was the most people Ursula had seen in one place in many years, maybe forever, and she had to stop and steady herself to avoid getting dizzy.

They passed sellers of beaded jewelry and spools of yarn. Others sold dried meats and even jars of preserves. The smell of the most beautiful incense wafted through the place, a jasmine and fresh rain scent. Someone played music on an old record player, like her father used to, and at once she was back by her old fireplace, reading Shakespeare.

Cutter led her clockwise to the other side of the town square. The hallways around the edges fanned out like spokes on a wheel, facilitating the movement of all the people as they came and went. These concrete halls were much bigger than the synthetic ones containing the ghastly science experiments. These were part of the old sewer systems, more like roads, with plenty of room for traffic to flow in both directions.

Cutter explained how they had converted it from an underground government facility that had been evacuated and abandoned during the blackouts. When the federal government splintered into sects across different cities around the country, this space became theirs for the taking.

"And what about the people in the vats?" Ursula asked.

"Not our proudest collections," Cutter admitted. "But we didn't create them. We've just been studying the effects the radiation had on their bodies. From them, we're learning more and more about how the brain functions."

Ursula's room was a short walk from the town square, a one-room deal with a bed and a sink and a toilet. There were no windows, but she was grateful to find a small shelf full of books near the bed. A lightbulb dangling on a chain overhead would provide enough light to read.

Cutter handed her a key. "You can come and go as you please. But get some sleep tonight, I'll be back in the morning so we can begin."

"Begin what?"

"What your father trained you to do."

"And what is that?"

Cutter blinked. "To win the war. To kill that fucking brain."

10
URSULA'S FATE REVEALED

THE NEXT MORNING URSULA WAS AWAKENED BY THREE dings from a bell outside her door. The owner of the bell went up and down the hall, from room to room: the wake-up call for the officials of the underground city. It was 6 a.m.

After a breakfast of oats and watery coffee, Cutter led Ursula to the conference room. Twelve seats surrounded a metal table. The young woman sat in her own chair in the corner, taking it all in. To an outsider, she might have exhibited the cold, hard stare of a condemned prisoner.

In reality, she was only meditating on her situation. She now knew her father had trained her so she could take down the brain. But how? What did the rebels expect her to do?

Her loneliness and despair began to mount. Losing her father, the journey, the violence, the poisoning, and now the overload of all these people, her revealed mission . . . it was too much.

So engrossed in her thoughts, she didn't notice as the seats began to fill.

Cutter sat with the other eleven council members, six

men and six women in total. The meeting was convened. A servant brought in jugs of water; in the corner a stenographer took notes.

Ursula sat like an odd duck and shifted in her seat.

"As you all discovered this morning, this girl's father had been an asset to us for over a decade. His intelligence provided the rebellion with detailed information that saved countless lives east at Fort Wilderness. Before his death, I arranged for his daughter to stay with us."

"More of Dean's ridiculous experiments?"

A bald man in a full-white, neck-high one-piece suit stood. His name was Majestic.

"All we heard from Dean for years," he said, "was of battling the brain with . . . what was it? Telepathy?"

The rest of the room tittered.

"I know we haven't agreed on how to handle the brain," said Cutter, "but while you and your crew struggled to deliver even a single viable weapon to penetrate its outer electromagnetic force field, Dean and I believed we could circumvent that altogether. In fact, there *is* a way."

"Telepathy is bollocks," said Majestic. "It's about science. Atoms. Molecules. Force."

In response, Cutter turned to her presentation. "For five years, Dean fed us information about the experiments in the government labs."

She clicked into the next slide. The cover page of an official study bore the seal of One-State in the upper-right corner. Its title read, "Study suggests ideal conditions for ex vivo communication between Homo sapiens and Cerebri materia."

"The paper's author, Herod Peck. Obsessive. Compulsive. Some insiders have compared him to Dr.

Frankenstein. He's convinced of theories such as black hole energy and source-field harnessing. He once spent three weeks holding yogic postures in the belief he could invoke the levitation of everyday objects.

"Ridiculous theories, I'll admit. However, all of us, I'm sure, would have once thought a floating brain that emerges only at night, with no visible means of flight, to be ridiculous as well. And I believe Herod Peck made the find of a lifetime. Something that everyone missed, or was too afraid to consider.

"We know the brain grew massively from the radioactive energy after the nuclear meltdowns." She gestured to the marked locations in the presentation. "And we know it uses the electromagnetic fields of the earth to float above ground and protect itself from every weapon we have thrown at it. It was once thought impossible, but we've all seen it in action. We believe the radiation has altered its synapses to make it capable of interfacing with energy fields in a way we've never been able to. Never even *dreamed* of being able to," she added.

"So your thesis is that Herod has found some way to talk to the brain?"

"If the brain is using electromagnetic radiation as a kind of channel to interface with energy fields," Cutter said, "then why couldn't Herod use the same channel to speak to it?"

She clicked into the next slide. A faded picture of Herod in a classroom writing on a dirty chalkboard. Sleeves rolled to his forearms, covered in dust.

"Dean Kent believed that Herod found the precise mix of chemicals and circumstances to transform his own brain's wavelengths to match those of the brain." A series of complex equations appeared on-screen. "These are the formulas Herod developed to isolate the wavelength and effect communication between a human brain and the floating one. His theory was that he could create a 'mind-pipe' that connected two or more people to the same electromagnetic hub, where communications were instant and free-flowing. The key was implanting a third eye. Herod had not only discovered the means by which to create a mind-pipe, but he had plugged himself into it via the eye. And it worked.

"So Dean prepared himself for the same medical procedures, to follow Herod into the mind-pipe. Only someone as powerful as Herod, he thought, would be able to defeat him, and the brain.

"But Dean figured rightly that his days were numbered. It was only a matter of time before the authorities discovered the source of the information leaks. Someone else had to be able to follow his work, in case he didn't make it.

"There was another consideration then. The candidate. The human mind is very powerful. It's able to force out, or keep at bay, ideas and thoughts it finds objectionable. Denial, for instance, is almost impossible to contend with.

"So, he decided, an adult with a fixed mind would simply not do."

She gestured to Ursula, who was sitting there, very still, eyes closed, arms crossed, the girl who hated this, all of it, who wished for the simple days of training and reading.

"He trained his daughter, day in and day out, to give her impeccable control over her thoughts and actions. To steel herself, to make herself emotionally resilient. Mind and body, together as one. To replace him if he did not make it.

"Don't look so surprised. As if all of you hadn't figured it out by now. This young lady is the one who is going to implant a third eye into her skull and engage the brain in psychic warfare. She is our only hope of winning this war."

II
HEROD'S RECOVERY

HE WOKE UP TWO DAYS AFTER THE BURSTING OF THE mind-pipe, sooner than he expected, but still in a state of nerve-racking shock.

Herod took no food, only water, for another two. Rehabilitation required deep stretching; the spasms locked him up so bad he could hardly move from bed without a nasty bite of pain. Meditation three times a day, an hour per session, helped him regain some feeling of normalcy.

It also helped calm the eye.

Years prior, he found that with a sound and sober mind he could easily control the eye. The external organ merely needed a different kind of attention than the rest of the body. Whereas most human functions run more or less autonomously, a foreign object like a radioactive eye hooked directly into the pineal gland takes an extraordinary amount of support to function properly.

For example, he needed to ingest more fat than normal to stay strong and healthy. He had told the government, while securing funding for the implant: "The older mystics claimed that in order to stay open, the pineal gland must be devoid of animal fat. That may have been true, but they weren't working with an implanted, radioactive eyeball.

"In this case, in order to keep the eye comfortable and content in its new home, I'll need all the animal fat I can get. Yes, meat is a delicacy these days, but without it I cannot feed the eye inside me. It needs an overdose of B-vitamins that I cannot find elsewhere."

The most nutrient-dense animal parts are typically the organs—the kidneys, the liver, the pancreas. Few cared to eat those anyway, which had helped Herod secure his fill. Pig brain, he found, lightly baked, seemed to energize the eye.

A week after the bursting of the mind-pipe, Herod put on his best suit and left his apartment for the first time. Stepping outside, he felt the familiar pang in his forehead—the cold wind nipping the eye, producing a shudder. Some days he wished he never had embarked on this journey, never followed through with the implant. Now he had no choice; he could never remove it safely. He would die taking it out. Besides, for a man like him, without the pursuit of harnessing the most overwhelming forces in all of the universe—gravity and electromagnetic energy—what was the point of living?

COUNCILMEMBER KAPLAN WAS NOT PLEASED HE HAD LOST the girl. Not pleased at all.

He sat there stonily as Herod gave him the update.

His mind was on other things.

Like how if those living inside the cities knew the extent to which the government was secretly controlling the brain—if *that* secret ever got out—they might lose control of the population overnight.

"We aren't controlling the brain, sir," interrupted Herod.

"Fine. Influencing it." Kaplan stood and paced the room. He was a large man, and already sweating. "You and I and the whole operation will be finished. There would be a mass revolt. Right now, the population lives in quiet fear inside the cities. The brains patrolling the Outerlands are the external threats we need to bring law and order to our country. People are free to leave the cities any time they want, but they will be at the mercy of the brain. It's a delicate balance we have to maintain after the collapse."

"Politics don't interest me," said Herod. "Only science and the brain. I'll leave the rest up to you."

"Politics is a matter of stories, and people understand them. I've been hearing a story myself that's interesting. Would you like to hear it?"

Herod stared at him.

"The story is that Dean Kent had always kept his daughter, Ursula, under tight wraps. Cared about her more than life itself. Trained her to be of sound mind and body. Now he is dead. But where is the girl? And what was he preparing her for?"

Herod froze. He could tell where this was going. And he didn't like it.

"Now she's gone," Kaplan said. "She's gone and you've been in some kind of accident. The park, I hear, is in disarray. A vagrant was vaporized."

Herod swallowed. "Sir, it's true that Ursula Kent is missing. But we will recover her soon, and I see no reason to worry—"

"Worry? Worry! You know what I think, Herod? I think Kent created an heir. Everything he learned from work, he came home and trained her. Day in, day out.

"Now the one person who could bring down our system is on the run, and you let her get away."

"We're close," Herod said to his superior. "We will recover the girl. Quickly."

"I hope so," said Kaplan. "Because if I were the rebels, I would be preparing her for the procedure right now. Find her before she's activated," he said. "Or I'm terminating your little experiments. And after that, I'll terminate you."

THAT PRICK.

Herod flushed red as he swept through the hall and up to the lab. He needed time to think.

Two things he had to figure out. First, obviously, the location of the girl. Second, what she was doing there. From his previous session with Ditsch, he had gotten her initial destination in the park. He cursed himself for the emotionalism when he tore out the rest of the robo-man's wires.

Clicking on the light above his worktable, he spread out the map and browsed the general area where Ursula had disappeared. Just west was the forest where the blast had come from.

Someone had helped her. Someone had distracted the brain while others had swooped in to save her.

Or, was it possible that the brain had doubled back and killed the girl after Herod had been torn from the mind-pipe? What if she was already dead?

There was no way to know. He wasn't about to effect contact with the brain again, not in his still-fragile state. And there was no way to know the exact location of where she was hiding if she was alive.

Though Herod had a good guess.

He pored once more over the map. The closest spot, arguably the best spot, to hide would be in the underground city north of the Barrows. The government, of course, knew the city was there, though as long as the rebels didn't cause trouble they weren't harassed. But if members of the city were the ones who had shot the brain as a distraction, then they were causing trouble, weren't they? And there was a good chance they'd have taken the girl back to their hideout.

It would be difficult to mount an incursion into the underground city on such short notice. No doubt they were already prepping the girl for her mission.

Which might be a good thing, Herod realized. It would save him lots of trouble later on if they readied her for her implant now . . .

Yes.

At once, he knew what to do. He would let them work on her, put her in place to go and destroy the brain herself. And then he would . . .

Herod had his plan. He sat back in his chair and caught his breath. The eye, sensing his excitement, poked out of his skull in anticipation.

He decided to give himself one good night's sleep. He would need the rest to prepare—for the fight of his life.

12.

URSULA'S DECISION

SHE COULDN'T BREATHE. HER WHOLE BODY WAS NUMB AND tingly, the eyes of the twelve council members leering at her like cats ready to pounce. Cold sweat running down her back, she quietly excused herself from the meeting where these adults so casually discussed her fate.

Once out the door, she ran.

URSULA CRAWLED UP AND OUT OF THE SEWER. SEEING nothing but brown hills ahead, she leapt up and raced away. She crested over many knolls in a dead sprint, until she saw something in a valley below. Following the remnants of a broken trail down the slope, she soon stood in an old street which had long since been overrun by the elements.

A ghost town, she realized. It must have been abandoned years ago. Skeletal buildings loomed on either side of the road, crusty with soot from an ancient fire. Forgotten cars, buried in mounds of dirt, made odd shapes in the street.

She wandered for an hour or so, in and out of the buildings. There was a pharmacy, a supermarket, a library, all raided. More exciting to her were the series of homes set back from the main drag. She was delighted to find that most of them still had their doors and windows.

She stepped onto the porch of a beautiful two-story home. Sitting on the rusty swing she looked from one end of the porch to the other, the length of the house, admiring the view as if the house were her own. This is what it could be like, sitting here after a long day, with no one trying to control her. Where she could just be herself, and do what she wanted.

Space. There was space here. It filled her heart. She could breathe easier. Growing up in a government high-rise, her whole life prescribed to her from day one, she longed for expansion, and the ability to make . . .

something. She wasn't sure what. A family? A life? Was it even possible anymore?

She resumed walking, catching her reflection in the grimy window of a remaining storefront. Hair, mussed and wild, stringy and dry and nasty, whipped around in the wind. Her shirt was torn in a few places. She felt old, like she'd been aged prematurely.

They'll never leave you alone, she thought. You can't go home, that's for sure. You can't stay outside; the brain will find you sooner or later. And the rebels, this Cutter and all the rest of them . . . they'll never let you just live either.

She felt a sense of righteous anger flow through her. No one had ever asked her what she wanted for herself. It had all been foisted upon her. Her life had never been hers. Not really.

You've been bred. Like an animal.

She'd given her whole life to a cause she'd never asked to fight. There, in the dust, she cursed her father, the rebels, the world.

And if there was no going home, and if the government would never stop hunting her, and if the rebels would never stop hounding her, and if the brain would never stop roaming, then she would never be free. Not until she did something.

It's up to you now, she told herself. To create your own life.

Whatever that might end up being. All she knew was she wanted it to be her own. Away from the government. Away from the rebellion. Away from the brain.

Then and there she made a pact with herself. From now on, her life would be hers to live, and hers alone. Never again would she fulfill anyone else's dreams.

But there was a price to pay for this new life. She knew that. That price was combat. Combat with the brain and with the government. And, if it came down to it, with the rebels. She may never have had a choice before, but now she saw the choice was hers.

She gave herself another hour to daydream, to start constructing her new life in her mind, and when the sun began to fade, she went back across the hills and into the sewers, quietly and without regret.

13

IMPLANTATION

IT LOOKS SO ORDINARY, URSULA THOUGHT. JUST LIKE A normal eye.

They were standing in an underground lab. The ultraviolet lights above had hurt her eyes until they gave her the proper glasses. Everything still swam blue, but at least she no longer hurt.

Ursula stepped up to the clear tank of liquid and peered at the floating eye. The optic nerve was still attached; it lagged under the eyeball like a wet piece of yarn.

"So let me get this straight. You want me to let you implant *this* in my head. So I can talk to the brain?"

"In a sense. None of us knows what communicating with the brain will be like. It could be like talking, but our hunch is that it's more like envisioning, or emoting even."

Ursula ran her finger over the glass. The iris of the eye was like a clear blue ocean.

"The eye should link up fine with your system," said Cutter, "but once it's implanted, it will use your brain the way a device uses a battery. You will be responsible not only for your health and wellbeing, but the eye's as well. When it's unhappy, you will know. A strict diet of meat and vitamins will help. It needs fat. It craves it.

"Remember though, that you're the more powerful one. You're the one who tames it. Your thoughts and concentration help *focus* it. You're the power source."

All her previous training made sense in light of the information she'd learned over the past few days. The endless mental exercises, the equations, the meditations and memory challenges. Her father had never told her why, exactly, he'd trained her that way. And, like a good little girl, she'd never even asked. But it was all in preparation for the implantation of the third eye.

Still, if she was honest with herself, she had to admit she liked all the training and exercises. It had given her a sense of pride and accomplishment. Her father had once told her how children growing up way back when used to sit in front of screens with images in them that moved around. They spent their whole lives that way. Entire industries had been built on providing the images. The pictures had numbed them, deadened them to their inner lives. But not her. She lived in the real world.

From her third eye would emerge a new sixth sense. Maybe that's what those people were trying to achieve with their screens, she thought. Maybe they'd been trying to bridge realities, to connect with others through a common place of sound and vision and emotion.

Her connection, though, would be the real thing.

Albeit with a giant disembodied brain.

She remembered closing her eyes before the operation—and then she blinked them open, though she couldn't see yet. She tried lifting her hands, but they were strapped to her sides. It was for her own protection, they said. The bandages around her head had to stay on—to keep the eye docile—and no one was about to chance Ursula accidentally swiping them away.

For three days she remained in her straps, swimming in and out of consciousness, aware of her state but too groggy to fight it. Much too groggy. Finally they let her unwrap the bandages around her two normal eyes. But it would be two more days before they let her walk.

The layers of gauze around her forehead were to come off slowly—one at a time over the course of a week or so, to let the eye acclimate to any light that peeked through. Any faster than that, they said, would risk an accident. It was hooked straight into her brain, after all.

She started her new diet of meat and green vegetables. The worst part of her meal plan was the noxious, muddy tonic they made her drink daily, some mixture of vitamins and minerals that tasted like dirt and turned acidic in her stomach.

Little by little, she grew accustomed to her new life, until the final bandage was removed.

She shuddered as she looked.

"Don't be scared," said Cutter. "It's part of you now."

The girl slowly turned back to the mirror.

The eye rested in the indented cavity in her forehead. It was bright blue, the sclera red and agitated. It had no eyelashes—or eyelids. To keep it moist, she'd have to keep it covered with the flap of skin that hung down.

It's disgusting. She winced at the sight of the eye. *It's repulsive.* It just sat in there, peering out, moving from side to side a little, taking in its new surroundings. She felt she'd been grafted with some alien creature, a parasite. She wanted to vomit.

"It's nausea," Cutter said. "The eye is reacting, putting pressure on you and causing a small migraine. It will pass."

It eventually did, and Ursula spent another week acclimating the eye to normal life. She took daily trips out of the sewer and up to the surface. The eye tolerated the sunlight well; it enjoyed the vitamin D.

She found she had developed a heightened sense of intuition, an ability to "see" in a different way. People became more complex; she perceived greater depths within them. They had an internal glow she'd never noticed. She seemed to know what they were feeling or thinking, though she never told them so and wouldn't have been able to explain it fully if she had.

Once an intuitive thought was fully formed, she found if she pushed a little with her mind, the other person was more . . . suggestible. Without speaking, she "told" an assistant what she wanted for dinner. The assistant immediately left the room and returned with a plate of chicken breast and broccoli. They never said a word to each other.

Ursula also returned to her daily routine, the one her father set down for her long ago. She awoke promptly at 6 a.m. and went above ground to meditate in the rising sun. There was no ice bath, so she meditated for one hour instead of her usual twenty minutes. She followed a breakfast of meat and eggs with memory exercises. She gradually worked in psychic activities with a deck of cards: reading them from behind, or shuffling the deck and listing off each card in order without seeing them.

One day she and Cutter were enjoying a little sun during lunch. "You tried implanting others before," Ursula said abruptly, reading her mind. "But the procedure didn't work. What happened?"

Cutter looked at her with lifted brow. There was no point in lying. "Yes, we tried a few times. But the subjects couldn't control the eye. Instead, it controlled them. On its own, the eye can't regulate a human body. It doesn't want to, and it doesn't know how."

"Because it uses the body like a battery."

"Exactly. And if the person can't control it, it feeds off the mind. The person's psyche, you see. The eye will eat their ego and their sense of self. It happens in fragments, like disintegrating links in a chain. Slowly the person breaks down."

"That's what happened to the rest of them?" Ursula asked.

"Yes. Nobody wore an eye for more than three days before you. But we knew you would respond well to it. Your father's training assured that."

A breeze blew through. Ursula leaned her head back and let it lift her hair. She felt the eye poke itself out of her head, like a gopher in a hole, stretching toward the wind and the light.

It was delighted.

14
Ditsch Lives

The awakening came in fits and starts, like the flickering of a light.

After his torture session, Ditsch had been tossed in the trash bin, his parts to be recycled into some new robo-man somewhere down the line.

By a stroke of luck, a tech in the smelting center had plugged him in to test his charger and a few parts, to see what could be salvaged. But a shipment arrived that stole his attention, and soon boxes were piled up around the robot. Ditsch was hidden for days.

Under normal circumstances he would have been fully operational within a few hours of charging, but due to energy constraints electricity was being diverted to other areas. The only electricity Ditsch received were the tiny bursts here and there as the circuit breakers switched every few hours.

Yet even in those small increments, he remembered.

He'd been tortured. Wires torn and discarded. Surgically, expertly, ripped apart.

His computer chips were still intact, his motherboard whole. All he lacked now were the internal wires to hook up the synthetic equivalent of his nervous system—the power unit of the whole mechanism.

Robo-men had never been designed to think for themselves. They were certainly not designed to think their way toward evolution. But Ditsch was no ordinary robo-man. Indeed, nothing and nobody who worked with Dean Kent had been ordinary, for Dean had a way of turning everyone super in some way.

Consistent with the philosophy he brought to teaching his daughter, he'd educated Ditsch early on in his own anatomy. Why this wire ran to that connector, how electrons leapt through the silicon, and, most importantly, how to route electricity to his base-power unit from other body parts.

Dean had several peculiar ideas he'd put to work on Ditsch. One was that robo-men should exercise. He suspected it would help them observe how power flowed to and from their terminals, which motors and cables might swell with the heat generated, and so on. It was a novel idea. No one had ever thought of teaching a robo-man to run. What purpose could it have served?

But Dean *had* thought of it. And as Ditsch exercised, it was discovered he could "feel" those connections. In fact, it was easy to tell what was overheating, and when, and how to reroute electricity as needed to conserve power or even cool himself down.

Two other incredible developments took place. The first was that Ditsch *preferred* exercising to remaining stationary. Though he had to be careful of how fast he went, he could run for up to twenty-four hours at a time under proper conditions. He enjoyed the feeling in his body, the control he had over it, the way the heat loosened up his silicone legs.

The second development would have been inconceivable to the government bureaucrats.

It had to do with love.

Ditsch came to realize that when Dean and Ursula spent time with him—and sometimes when they gently set a hand on his shoulder—he noticed a certain set of wires that flowed to his power unit surging with energy, jolting his body in a way he grew to find comforting. He appreciated their compliments. In fact, he could recall no experience with either his pseudo-progenitor or his daughter that he found displeasing.

Over the years, whether due to his circuitry or something like genuine emotion, Ditsch began to love them both in his own way. Perhaps similar to the way a baby wants to be close to its parents, an emptiness inside him filled when they were near.

Science, it turned out, didn't know everything.

DITSCH WAS ABLE TO SUM UP HIS ENTIRE SITUATION WITH just a few moments of electricity. Every microsecond he had, he scanned his body for the connections that needed fixing, then rerouted power to the available circuits.

In a minute (over many days) he had identified where and how to split electricity between circuits to allow him enough power to stand and walk to the portable generator on the table across the room. He would have only a few moments to hook himself in before his energy was depleted, but once he was connected and the generator turned on, he would have all the time he'd need to fix himself up.

It was time for Ditsch to go.

WHEN THE TECH RETURNED LATER THAT EVENING, HE suddenly got a funny feeling. Something inside him told him to remain silent.

He could hear some tinkering around the corner, and as he peeked he saw what appeared to be a robo-man standing in front of the giant mirror. His chest was flayed open, both sides stretched and held by clamps attached to metal stands.

Little sparks ricocheted here and there, as the robo-man soldered himself back together.

The tech froze. Any robot capable of bringing itself back to life like that was not to be messed with. He backed further into the shadows and watched.

Minutes later, the robo-man unhooked himself from the clamps and stitched his outer shell back together.

Then he leaned down, tied his shoes, and left the building.

The tech quietly followed the robo-man, gently catching the door before it closed. He stuck his head out and watched as Ditsch calibrated his direction.

Then the robot bolted out into the open Outerlands.

The tech went back inside. Far be it from him to tell Herod his plastic creature had escaped from the smelting station.

So he went inside and filled out a report that said Ditsch had been destroyed by fire weeks before, then went to work and never told a soul.

The robo-man, meanwhile, went running.

15

RECONNAISSANCE, WITH A TWIST

WHEN DEAN KENT TAUGHT HIS DAUGHTER ABOUT warfare, he quoted a Confederate horseman named Nathan Bedford Forrest. To win, one should "Get there first with the most." It meant, he said, that you had to get there physically, get there before the enemy, and get there with the most men.

Ursula remembered this as she and Cutter rode out to the edge of the tree line ten miles from the underground city to scout a good spot for the upcoming fight with the brain. They'd never have enough soldiers, but that wasn't what she was counting on to win. Beyond the border marked by the tree line was nothing but miles and miles of scorched soil. They parked the electric bike and watched the dust swirl.

Cutter decided the battle between Ursula and the brain should take place here, where, if she had to, Ursula could take cover under the foliage.

They stared west until Cutter started the electric bike. "Come on. Time to start heading back. It'll be dark soon."

Silence, for several moments. Then Ursula turned. Cutter shuddered as the third eye, protruding a half-inch from the girl's head, stared back at her.

"Change of plans." Ursula pointed west. "Take me that way."

"We're too far from the base. We don't have time. The bike will be out of juice—"

"The brain sleeps that way. We're going now."

"The *plan*," Cutter emphasized, "is to come back tomorrow night with the crew. We have to stick to the plan."

"No."

"No? Why not?"

Ursula stood very still, the eye panning left to right. "The brain knows we're coming. The government knows, too. We have to surprise it tonight. It's the only way to gain an advantage."

Cutter shook her head. "But we don't know where it is. The bike will run out of power before we find it."

"Not today."

The girl looked to be in some kind of trance. Cutter would have to explain this slowly. "These bikes are only good for a few hours' of riding. The batteries need to be charged."

"Yes," the girl said, "they can't hold a charge on their own."

"That's right." Cutter waited for her point.

"And until today, you've never had a portable source of power to keep the bikes running. But now we do."

The eye focused on Cutter, bulging, the sclera red with irritation, the gaze steady with intention. And purpose. And drive. Cutter couldn't break her stare. The eye drew her in.

Cutter got the hint first, the realization second. The hint was yes, the brain and the girl were going ahead. Cutter could either stay there or go with them. To stay there, in the middle of nowhere with no bike and no supplies, meant death.

The realization of how they would continue hit her second.

The eye was a transmitter, and the girl was the battery. The girl would provide the energy to the eye, who would route it to the bike. How, Cutter couldn't figure out.

If she were asked, Ursula wouldn't have known how it worked either, only that it could. And it would.

Without a word, Cutter climbed onto the back of the bike, holding on to Ursula's jacket.

Soon they were off, setting out for the hazy horizon where only the faint glimpse of mountainous rock was seen, inside which the brain was fast asleep.

16

THE HUNT

HOURS LATER, THE BIKE'S MOTOR SHOWED NO LACK OF power or performance, but even so Cutter was nervous. The tires were balding, worn nearly past their tread. One sharp cactus spike, or a jagged rock, and they could be stuck out here.

Yet they cruised on, the older woman's arms around the young lady's waist, into the wasteland. Nothing living in sight. She guided Ursula along, reading the compass, recalling everything the rebels knew about where the brain went at night.

They didn't know all that much.

Of the three other attempts to track the brain, the first two never made it past the lone tree before being zapped by the brain.

Then they sent Pieter Volkov, the Russian expat, on foot to follow the creature and report back. As an outdoorsman, he had taken many teams across the most dangerous terrain in America to deliver supplies, hunt game, or assassinate an unlucky warlord. He returned after three weeks, full of holes from the brain's poison spittle and babbling insanities. He died of his wounds shortly after.

Since then, Cutter hadn't received approval from the council to send a new crew.

Over time, in the presence of other pressing matters, Cutter had forgotten about defeating the brain. It wasn't a priority for the council; it was something they just lived with.

Not until Dean had established contact and given them the blueprints for the third eye implant.

She certainly never thought *she* would be the one chosen to help do battle. Not clinging to a young girl on the back of an electric bike powered by psychism.

The sun was going down by the time they reached the stony pathway that weaved between rock formations on either side. Ursula hopped off the bike, staring ahead as if making a reading. She turned back and threw her head in the direction of the path, motioning to Cutter, and started to walk.

Cutter placed the bike next to the lone surviving chaparral and followed, their footsteps echoing together in the canyon. They walked for thirty minutes in the narrow bottom where the sunlight no longer reached.

Suddenly they were hit by a stench that made Ursula gag and double over. It was worse than the smell of the group of rats that had died under their stairwell that one time when she was seven, more awful than the gangrene on a soldier's leg her father had treated at home. She still remembered the stink of rotting cheese.

They were approaching the lair of the floating brain.

Cutter fashioned a bandanna out of a salve sheet. She tore it into two strips and handed one to Ursula, who took it with gratitude and tied it around her head.

As they penetrated deeper into the canyon, the walls on either side began to slope inward; it felt as if the rocks were closing in on them overhead. Soon they entered a dark tunnel. The sky disappeared.

The stench grew exponentially worse. It smelled like rancid fish stuffed in a camel and left in the sun, an open city sewer piped into a home, worse than a—

Ursula threw up again.

THE TRAIL CONTINUED TO NARROW UNTIL THEY WERE pushing through a slit in the rock the size of a bedroom door. They entered the dark cavern; a few paces in, Ursula felt herself slip and fall backward. Her butt hit the ground and then she slid down a slick chute. Frantically she scrabbled to find something to hold onto, yet all she found was Cutter, behind her. Gathering speed, they slid faster and faster, until they felt a sudden weightlessness and were spilled onto the rocky floor.

Ursula stood, dusting herself off—when her breath choked in her throat. She grabbed Cutter's hand in a cold death grip. They stared with open mouths at the floating brain the size of a house in the center of the large hexagonal space, on the ground. A few hundred feet above them loomed a large hole with a view of the night sky.

The brain's eyes were closed. It emitted tiny breaths accompanied by green bubbles from its flat nose.

It appeared to be sleeping.

Ursula could see the pulsating patterns of gray matter, the blue veins that zig-zagged its circumference like rivers on a map. Ooze dripped from every indent, every pockmark; the thing was a gelatinous glop, shiny and moist. Its tentacles were splayed on the floor below, twitching in languor as the thing slept.

Cutter backed away instinctively, tugging on Ursula's arm.

But the young lady shook her head.

She wasn't leaving.

Instead, she sat on the cool stone floor, closed her eyes, and began to meditate.

FOCUSING ON THE PNEUMATIC SOUND OF THE BRAIN'S breathing, Ursula established her own breath in sync. She held the inhales, tensing specific sets of muscles and releasing them on the exhale. First she tensed and relaxed her head, then her neck and upper shoulders. Then the chest and so on. She worked her way down her body, on each breath out squeezing out all the tension, visualizing her stress dissipating before moving on to the next area.

She imagined her in-breath bringing a wave of pure

white air into her nostrils, whirling her thoughts into a tiny tornado that gathered impurities as it wound through her body, before she pushed it all out. In this way, she cleared her mind of all thoughts quickly and without much effort.

When the moon peeked out overhead through the top of the cave, Ursula stood and opened her eyes.

Motioning Cutter to stand back and stay hidden, she unwound the cover from over her third eye.

Her new eye blinked twice and opened.

It was time.

The brain blinked its eyes a few times before keeping them open. It nearly jumped when it saw the young woman, feet spread, arms jutting down, in an offensive stance. Fixing upon her, the brain rose.

Ursula stared back, bracing herself.

Cutter slipped back into the shadows.

And then all hell broke loose.

17

Psychotronic Death Match

Ursula hadn't known what to expect from herself when engaging in heavy psychic warfare, but when the time came, and all conscious thought left her, her body and mind seemed to know what to do. She had to trust it.

Stay tight. Focused. All energy upon it.

She repeated it to herself like a mantra, as she locked her three eyes onto the thing.

Hazy lines, currents of electricity, formed in the air

between them, emanating from their heads and meeting in the middle, wrapping around each other until they formed a strengthening coil.

Then the currents grew in intensity and size until they formed the rough walls of a tubelike structure.

The mind-pipe had been formed.

After several breathless moments, the surrounding rocks began to undulate.

So focused was Ursula that she hardly noticed the shifting all around her. Vibrations underfoot, she began to rise several inches off the ground.

Her head felt like an overfilled balloon. She so badly wanted to let it topple backward, dragging her with it, so she could simply rest. She'd never wanted to sleep so badly.

Yet she continued tightening her focus, repeating her mantra, and let her first burst of energy pulse through the mind-pipe and into the brain, an opening salvo of battle.

In response, the brain reared back and flung a torrent of energy.

Ursula was rocked by a bright yellow light; across her mind flitted sick, demented images. She saw her father's face, beaten, bloody, his body being dumped unceremoniously into the polluted river.

She screamed for him. She loved her father. She needed her father.

But her father was dead, and she was alive.

The violence of the nuclear blasts, so long ago, played out in mere seconds that felt like decades. She saw the initial explosions, the pulsing waves of destruction massacring families and children, their homes and lives swept up like dust with a broom. And the brain, in the aftermath, sweeping across the lands, crunching and slurping humans as they went down its grisly hatch. All she could do was watch.

The brain had captured and stored every bit of destruction, every bit of sadness and terror felt by the people it had eaten. That's what it feeds on, she realized. It feeds on the psychic pain, on the horror, of its victims.

Gritting her teeth, she dug her feet into the electric edges of the mind-pipe she now found herself standing on. She forced, with all her concentration, the freakish images back through the mind-pipe, at the brain.

It seemed to help. For a few seconds.

But the images crowded her in. Piling up, each behind the last, like a throng of looters against a plate-glass window. Soon it would shatter, and they would be upon her.

She would shatter.

It was too much. How could she have ever thought she'd win in mind-to-mind combat with this beast?

The psychotronic images of beaten men, raped women, burning babies, and chewed animals beat upon her. Gnarled people, twisted like vines, human heads atop horse bodies, with hooves for breasts, continued to screech.

Behind it all, the brain was grinning.

The images bludgeoned her like clubs. She felt her third eye squirming and bouncing off her skull, squealing, frantically trying to fend off the concentrated energy beams.

It might have been instinct, the steady years of meditation, but something told her, just when it was too much, as the pressure began to cave her in, simply, to quit.

She let the assault continue. Instead of fighting, she breathed through the images, inviting them in. Every last one.

She continued to breathe through her nose, gently envisioning sucking the pictures in through her nostrils. She gathered them up, drew them all into her breath, until they whipped into a little tornado inside her. At the apex of her breath, she wrapped the images tightly in her mind, compressing them down and down and down in size. A softball, a baseball, a six-sided die.

Then she let them go out through her mouth.

The mind-pipe warped and pulsed like a pressurized fire hose. The brain shrieked and recoiled as the energy wave hit. Red and blue sparks exploded on impact, searing and shredding its face. A slab of gray matter was flayed off its cheek.

Ursula screamed and let loose a second torrent, striking the brain between the eyes. It reeled back, the multicolor lightning bolts ricocheting off its face in all directions. A fissure appeared along the ceiling of the mind-pipe, splitting it in jagged sections, and on the next push the pipe shattered.

The explosion flung them in opposite directions, lifting Ursula and tossing her on the rock floor. She bounced hard once and landed on her back, gasping for air. Cutter ran for her, grabbed an arm and wrenched her to her feet, ready to throw her over a shoulder to escape the brain. Ursula stopped her.

"Wait. Look."

The brain had been thrown clear across the hexagonal rock floor, rolling to a stop on its side against the far wall. It was alive but badly beaten. Its veins still pulsed, albeit weaker and more sluggish than before.

It groaned, rolled over, faced them. Blood, from some kind of hemorrhage, had begun pooling in its eyes.

Ursula gathered all the residual energy she could find within herself. She turned it over in her mind—and belted the brain with it.

It shrieked, cowering deeper into the shadows. But it could find no escape from the wicked girl. It began to shrivel, the pockmarks dotting its face growing larger, looking as though it would collapse in on itself.

Ursula wound up for one final energy thrust, when she felt a vicious shove from behind. Flailing forward, she tried to break her fall but only half-succeeded; one arm folded under her as her weight drove her shoulder into the ground.

"That's enough."

Herod stood behind her, the moonlight streaming in blues and silvers from the hole above. He wore a black turtleneck and black pants and black boots that thudded on the stone as he approached her.

So this was him. The man chasing her.

"Yes, it's me," he said, reading her thoughts. "And you've done well. Better than we could have ever imagined."

He reached his hand out. She recoiled, crab-walking backward on her hands.

"If I wanted to kill you, I would have already," he said.

He was right. Still, she didn't trust him. Weak and weary, she helped herself up, standing beside Cutter.

Herod seemed to lose interest in them. He looked despondently at the brain. Its skin had begun to crack and dry out, its fluids almost completely dissipated. It had shrunk to nearly half its normal size, the giant fissures in its exterior fanning out across previously smooth gray matter.

He ran his finger over its back. Surprisingly, he wasn't hurt. No burning. No pain. The brain shuddered, its skin peeling away in flakes to the touch.

"A shame," he said. "He was our best one." He turned. "Now we'll have to create another." He paused. "Correction. You will."

"*Me?*"

"Your father was our best technician." He gestured to the brain. "This was his greatest work. His daughter should be able to follow suit."

"No," Ursula said, her face scrunching in disbelief. "He wouldn't do that."

"I'm afraid he did. It was he who started the experiments on human brains. Project X, we used to call it back then. His first attempts didn't work. Twelve in total. But this one, the thirteenth one, did."

He sighed. "Dean was different before he met your mother. He was undisciplined. Angry. A volatile combination in most people. It almost destroyed him. His genius was his saving grace.

"Back then, the rebels were even more hated by the cities than they are today. Your father loathed them. To him, it seemed all they wanted to do was destroy. To tear civilization down completely. He lost all respect for those outside the system. Especially after they burned his house down, before he moved into the apartment with your mother.

"The brain experiments started from his hatred, I think. There was one thing your father cared more about than anything else: Revenge. And he got it.

"When the experiment succeeded, the brains began

keeping guard over the Outerlands. There was our society —the official society—and the rebels. They lived there, we lived here. Anyone caught between was smoked by the brain."

Ursula frowned. Why was he telling her this? Why was this man, hell-bent on killing her, giving her this information about her father?

"I saw your father, as he grew older, the longer he was with your mother, begin to change. She was soft and gentle. And she gave him you. When she died, I believe he started having doubts. Doubts about what we had birthed. What he had so freely given the government.

"At some point, your father began sneaking secrets out—to *her*." He gestured to Cutter. "I thought we could work out some kind of deal with Dean," he said, "but we didn't have the time.

"Which brings us to you," he continued. "One snap of my finger and everyone will know the identity of the psychic girl who took down the brain. The rebels will want you for themselves. Bandits and thieves will hold you for ransom, or kill you if you give them trouble. If you leave here, you'll spend your whole life fending off the worst of the worst. Your future out here, among the rebels? I'm afraid you don't have one."

"What about you?" she said. "You don't want to kill me, or so you say. So what do you want?"

"I want you to come back with me."

"Why?"

"I'll give you any pay you want, any food you desire, any home you need. I'll give you all the protection the government can provide."

"For what?"

He smiled gently. "For managing the brains, of

course."

It was so simple, so matter-of-fact. It took Ursula a moment to register what she'd just heard. Manage the brains? Her?

"Like, talk to them?"

"Precisely."

"You don't need me for that."

"I do, actually. See, of all the things we humans have created, of all the miracles science has given us, we sadly cannot extend life. I'm old. I can feel time slipping away from me. But you're young. And more than capable. Soon you'll be more powerful than I could ever be. Yet, you see, you're not my enemy."

Ursula's veins ran cold like frosty rivers.

"Yes," he said, reading her mind. "You're my replacement."

Silence.

It made sense. She *was* the only person in the world who had actually taken down a brain. Conventional weapons had never worked against it; they could never penetrate its outer electromagnetic shell. But her mind had done the impossible. She had been trained, almost since birth, to interface with it. And if she could kill one, she could also communicate with—and control—the others.

Herod sat against the wall. He groaned in pain; all the standing had aggravated his arthritis. "Think of what it means," he said, "you'd be one of the most important people in the world. You would help keep order. Help run things. The world is too dangerous without order. We need you. *I* need you. And until he changed his mind, your father needed you too."

Silence fell over the rocky space as Ursula thought.

What would her life be like if she refused? If she spent the rest of her days—what, dodging government officials? Avoiding sketchy men in ragged trench coats in the sewers?

One truth was already clear to her: she was not from the world of the underground. She missed the comfort of the city. Soft sheets, good food. She never wanted for anything, not materially, and down underground there nothing was comfortable.

Her knees grew weak. She sat on the rocks and retreated inside herself to think, feeling like Odysseus trapped between Scylla and Charybdis, forced to choose the lesser of two evils. Herod didn't rush her. Instead, he closed his eyes and relaxed his head against the wall.

She contemplated this decision, this life with the government or the rebels, and presently found her mind turning back to the day she escaped the sewer, and ran, and found the ghost town, and the house, and the choice she'd made in the swirling dust out there.

And she knew.

She would let no government take her. And no underground either. She would be free. She would *choose* to be free. No matter if it meant fighting off officials and rebels for the rest of her life.

She smiled at Herod, the sweetest one she could muster.

Then she let the energy inside her fly.

HEROD KNEW, OF COURSE, WHAT HER DECISION WAS. HE sensed it easily, even before she knew herself. Young psychics, though powerful, are still young, and headstrong, and wear their feelings on their sleeves, more than enough for an experienced psychic to read.

In the instant before the girl released her energy, he pushed a gentle thought at her third eye. It was like those old comics he'd read as a kid. As the villain was about to fire a gun, the hero would slyly, unbeknownst to the villain, jam the barrel. When it was shot, it backfired.

The girl let out a little *oomph*, as the wind was sucked out of her. She flew back, her head slamming against the rock floor.

As he watched this young woman, her whole life ahead of her, gasping for air, a wave of sadness washed over him. Here she was, the most important young person in the country, maybe the planet, and she had little to no idea how powerful she could be. He would have killed for her power, her clarity, at her age. To have the world in the palm of his hand, to be young again, to be untouchable . . .

Ursula pushed herself up to her hands and knees. She was in a prime spot to listen to him, to understand him, to take a good, hard look at her life and her potential. Maybe he could get through to her.

But that was wishful thinking. She would never be all she could be—not in the way he wanted her to. There was too much rebellion inside her. Perhaps that could change as she grew up, as it so often did in others, but he didn't have years to wait her out.

What a waste.

As the girl stubbornly tried to rise, throwing every mind-energy wave she could at him, he knew that his dream was impossible.

So she had to go.

He sighed.

Gathering his mind-field, drawing in all available power, channeling his rage, frustration, his disappointment, his sadness, he concentrated everything he had into his third eye.

As he was about to let it loose, to shatter this young lady, he sensed a falling shape above him, the dim shadow slicing the silvery moonlight.

He looked up.

But by then it was too late.

18

Ditsch, from Above

The feeling the robo-man had while running could only be described as ecstasy.

The *plunk-plunk* of his feet pounding the earth, the kinetic motion, the hiss of gears turning, the sensation of sprinting so fast he was nearly out of control—Ditsch had achieved what no other robo-man had: a state of flow.

Underlying it all was his mission. His focus drove him. The sense of love for the girl he'd watched growing up drove him. And revenge for his fallen master drove him.

He had already computed the likely location of the brain. Years of logging and charting for Dean had given him a range to check of less than two hundred yards in diameter.

When he reached the corridor in the mountain—recalling that the brain would be underground during the day, and would need air above him to rise from the rock —he bypassed the route Ursula and Cutter took and raced straight to the rocks above.

He skidded to a stop just before the gaping hole.

Peering down, he saw the brain on its side, looking shrunken and damaged. There was Herod, way down there, with his hand raised and gathering a blue-yellow energy field from all around, preparing to strike.

If Ditsch were fully human, he might have gasped. His heart might have sunk at the young woman cowering on the rocks, steeling herself against the fatal blow that was sure to come.

But he had no heart, and he let out no gasp.

Instead, he acted. The girl he'd helped raise, his master's daughter, the most special person in the world. The one he'd made laugh, the one he'd seen cry. The one who must live now, for there had never been one like her, and never would be again.

The near-infinite calculations whirred inside him in less than half a second.

Then he spread his arms and leapt headfirst into the void.

HE FELL, LANDING ON HEROD'S CRACKLING HEAD FULL OF electric kindling, just as the third eye released the energy ball.

A single blast rocked everything, enveloping the room in a bright blue explosion. When it was over, only a crater remained where Herod had stood. There was no trace of him left. He had been completely vaporized.

All Ursula and Cutter found of the faithful robo-man was a charred, jagged piece of his motherboard.

Some call the motherboard the heart of every robot.

19
IT ENDS

TODAY THAT PIECE OF DITSCH SITS FRAMED IN THE museum, here in the old town that Ursula Kent made her home.

My grandmother would have liked to say her encounter with the brain was the one and only of her life—that she lived the rest of her days in the ease and quiet of town life.

But that's not what happened.

It would be thirty more years of struggle in turning the tide of the war against the brains and the government that backed them. And, at times, against the rebels too. I could tell many stories. Like the narrow underwater escape off the Atlantic coast, when she fought an ocean brain in submarine combat. The betrayal of the resistance that got her captured in New Texas and nearly burned at the stake as a witch. How she eventually destroyed all twenty of the remaining floating brains throughout the country.

I could tell you any dozen of stories. About her training, and her father, and the unlikely robot hero who sacrificed himself to save the world.

Like how she had my mother, and my mother had me.

Both of us, trained in the Mind Ways.

Yes, I could tell you many dozens of stories.

Maybe one day I will.

THE END.

Acknowledgements

Many thanks to those who read early drafts of these stories and provided notes, including Abby Cooper and Travis Schirmer. Thank you also to Karen Conlin for her editing, Jordan Harris for his cover design, and Hannah Nance for her cover titles.

"Chop" was inspired by Richard Matheson's short story, "Lemmings." All hail Richard.

The ending of "I'm Ready to Affirm You Now, Gamma" was inspired by Nigel Kneale's short story, "Tomato Cain." The title "Jack Nasty on the Wind" was inspired Nigel Kneale's story, "Jeremy in the Wind." All hail Nigel.

About the Author

Andrew Schrader is a Los Angeles-based author and filmmaker. In addition to directing feature films and music videos, he wrote several episodes of the animated show *Tig n' Seek* for Cartoon Network. He was also a script consultant on "Afterlife," the horror series from Crypt TV.

His three-book series, *What Goes On In The Walls at Night*, was featured on the Reddit No Sleep podcast and twice won the Red City Review Book of the Year for fantasy and horror.

Yes, of course he loves cats.

Read more at:
www.andrewjschrader.com